PLAYBOY'S HEART

NANA MALONE

COPYRIGHT

1

I swayed on my feet as I tried to remind myself that today was a shitty day to die.

Tell that to the burn in your side.

Funny thing was pain was a hell of a motivator. So was rage. He wanted to hurt what was mine. To take her from me. I might be a selfish asshole, but I would do whatever it took to protect my family.

I inspected my side and the slash of red peeking through my shirt. It stung like a whore's nails, but it was shallow. I'd live. The key was to make it through this and get home to Imani. "No one's looking for a fight. Maybe you have the wrong bloke."

The other man scoffed. "No, I think I have the right asshole. Did you really think I would give her up so easily? She fucking *belongs* to me. I gave her time to come home on her own, but now she thinks she's going to marry you? Fuck that. If she won't come willingly, I'm going to drag her ass back with me."

Imani? Fury flooded my veins, and I forced myself to take a deep breath. I had to stay in control. There was no way in hell I was letting this guy take Imani anywhere. She hadn't mentioned another ex besides Ryan. *Not like you've spent a lot of time talking about your pasts.* That was a good point. But if she had a homicidal ex, that was probably a good thing to mention *before* we'd slept together. "I don't know who you are, but I'm going to give you the chance to get the hell out of here. Imani isn't going anywhere with you. And if I see you around me or her again, it's going to be unpleasant for you. Are we clear, *mate?*"

The guy's brows drew down and furrowed. "Who the fuck is Imani? Is that what you're calling her now? Did she change her fucking name? I couldn't give a shit. I'll call her what I like. And all I'm clear on is that I'm taking Abbie home."

I faltered. *Abbie?* I'd assumed the homicidal arsehole was looking for me. But no, he was lying in wait for my brother. And Abbie.

Fuck. Abbie.

This was her ex, Easton. She hadn't gone into detail with me about the guy, just that she'd had a rough go of it. Lex had filled me in on the guy's more violent tendencies.

"You have the wrong bloke. But I'll do you a solid. If you get out of here now, I won't call the police to come collect you."

More with the furrowed brow. "You think you can make me leave? I'm not going anywhere without her."

As I cautiously stepped onto the barge, Easton rushed at me, intent on taking me out at the legs. Rolling onto the balls of my feet, I shifted my leg out of the way while snapping one hand around Easton's arm and the other around the back of his neck and aggressively assisted him facedown to the deck. For good measure, I delivered a punch, feeling the crunch of Easton's cheekbone under my knuckles.

Just like in training, I backed out of the way. "We don't have to do this." But the truth was I *wanted* to do this. This guy wanted to hurt Abbie. Wanted to hurt Lex. They were my fucking family. For once I wanted to be there for my brother.

Easton popped up, and his fingers gingerly touched his cheek as he glared at me.

He moved like a fighter.

Just my luck, but that was fine by me. It had been a while since I'd sparred, and I could use the workout. Easton sprang forward again with a straight punch. I deflected it by letting my left hand slide up his right arm and off-lining the punch. But Easton was quicker than he looked, and his knuckles grazed my eye.

I countered with my right, and Easton's head snapped back. With him exposed, I advanced with another punch to his throat. The fucker went down with both hands clutching his throat.

Stay down arsehole.

I could feel the tenuous strings of control snap. I wanted to kill him. Wanted him to hurt.

I hauled him into a more advantageous position with my left hand, then delivered punch after punch after punch. "You're not so big and tough now, when someone fights back, are you? You prefer someone small and help-less?" I hit him again, the rage taking over.

In my mind's eye, I could picture this guy taking his hand to Abbie. Then in my mind, Abbie was replaced by Imani. With a furious roar, I hit him again.

Eventually, Easton stopped flailing. It was only after he fell with a *thud* onto the wooden floor of the deck that I staggered back. The other man lay in a whimpering, moaning heap on the ground. Adrenaline and anger coursed through my veins, and my hands shook. I wanted to kill him. *Could* kill the guy. Nobody would miss him.

But if I did that, I'd never see Imani again. Or my brother. As it was, I'd probably gone too far, letting my emotions get the best of me.

Hands still shaking, I pulled my phone out and dialed 9-9-9. When the operator answered, I directed the police to the barge. Lex arrived just after I hung up.

"Fuck me, Xan, don't tell me you were on time for once, the one time I was—" My brother cut his words off short when he saw the man in a heap on the ground. "What the fuck?"

"Had a bit of a nasty surprise waiting when I got here."

"Jesus, Xan." Alexi gawked at me. "Is he alive?"

"Easy, baby brother. Don't you hear him moaning? Police are on their way."

Some of the tension rolled off Alexi's shoulders, and he studied me closely. "And you? All right?"

I glanced down at my hands. "Nothing a bucket of ice and a pint can't solve."

Lex narrowed his eyes. "Did he get you in the eye?"

I smirked. "Lucky hit."

"Who—"

Before he could finish asking, I cut him off. "That's Easton. I think he figured he could surprise you, or, even worse, Abbie. He was out of his mind, saying he was taking her back home with him."

Lex's usually calm demeanor slipped, and I saw something in him I hadn't seen in years, the will and the intent to do whatever it took to protect someone... even kill.

He lunged for the git, but I stepped into his path. "Easy, Lex. I took care of it. He's alive and the police are on their way. You have nothing to do here."

Lex shoved at my shoulders, but we were too evenly matched, and I stood my ground. "Not going to happen, so relax."

Alexi tried once more to move past me, but it was a half-hearted effort. "He would have killed her," he said, his voice wavering.

"Then aren't we all lucky that *I* was here instead? Abbie is safe, and you didn't have to dust off your rusty-ass Krav Maga skills."

My brother sneered. "I'm not rusty."

"Yeah, that's what I'm afraid of. If you had been here, he would be dead. Let me take care of you for once." I let the unspoken speak for itself. Alexi had killed once to protect me. There was no telling what he would do to protect the woman he loved.

The police came and took a statement, and an ambulance picked up what was left of a semi-conscious Easton as the police interviewed us. All the while, Lex remained quiet, speaking only when someone asked him a question. He provided the police with the security tape. But when he saw Easton's face, what I had done to him, Alexi gasped.

When the police left, Lex asked me softly, "You wanted to kill him, didn't you?"

I waited for the shame or guilt to wash through me, but it never came. "Yeah, but I didn't."

Alexi was quiet for a moment. "I'm grateful for what you did for her. When I think about what would have happened if she had been here…"

There was something that sounded like anguish in his voice, and I turned to face him. "I didn't just do it for her, Lex. If that had been you and he'd gotten the jump on you…"

Lex's next question was softer. "Do you still love her?"

A tight fist squeezed my gut. What the hell was I supposed to say to that? "I *do* love her." I scrubbed my hands over my face and winced at the sting of pain around my eye. "But not the way you think. She's family to me. Just like you are. No one touches my family without losing a pint of blood or two." I shrugged. "If he had hurt Imani, I would have done the same. Just like I know you would have."

Lex swallowed hard. "I—I'm grateful you were here."

"Me too."

⚜

IMANI

I let myself into our place with my brass key and smiled.

Careful now, it's just pretend.

Even if it was just pretend, I liked thinking of the flat as our place. Soon, I would go back to my normal life. I needed to call Felix tonight. He'd left for Ireland two days ago, and he wouldn't be back for another two days, so we were due for a catch-up. But I wouldn't be able to see him until the weekend if my rehearsal schedule kept up. I was way overbooked, but I'd find time. I missed my bestie.

When I let myself in, the lights in the kitchen were on low, but the living room was dark. Had I left them on? Had Xander turned them on for me remotely so I wouldn't come home to a dark house? He knew I had no idea how to work the remote security app. He'd taken to doing things like that for me. I didn't know what had changed, but after the club last weekend, he'd been different.

It was as if some invisible barrier between us had been torn down by force. If I didn't know better, I'd say he was the perfect boyfriend. He treated me exactly how I would want someone to treat me.

Except how much of that is real?

If any of it at all.

He'd said he was meeting Lex for a drink, so I didn't expect him for a while. Maybe I'd have some time to shave and do the girl thing. As I slipped my shoes off, I tossed my keys on the table in the foyer.

But when I reached for the light switch in the living room, a deep voice halted me. "Leave the light off, Imani."

My heart jumped as my adrenaline spiked, but I instantly quelled the panic. I knew that voice. "Xander? I thought you were hanging with Lex tonight. Why are you sitting in the dark?" I reached for the light switch again, and his voice got even deeper. "I said leave it off."

I stilled then licked my lips nervously. "Is everything okay?"

I dropped my bag on the kitchen counter.

"Come here."

Something wasn't right. Tentatively, I stepped toward the shadow on the couch. "Okay. You want to tell me what's going on?" When I reached the couch, I paused, unsure of what to do next.

"Closer."

My gaze slid to the floor so I could avoid any obstacles in my way. "Xander? You're freaking me out a little. What's the matter? Talk to me."

"What's the matter is I need you. Fuck now, talk later."

With a wave of his magic dick wand, heat pooled in my core, easily setting my blood on fire. As if I was the only one who could give him what he wanted. What he *needed*.

"Okay," I whispered, unsure of exactly what he wanted from me. "I'm here."

"Bend over the couch. Knees on the cushions. Brace your hands on the backrest."

"Uh…" My voice trailed off. I trusted him. Knew he wouldn't hurt me. I could refuse if I wanted to. Not that I wanted to.

I just had no idea what was prompting his current mood, and I was slow to comply. He didn't say a word, just waited patiently for me to do as he said. I started to shake as adrenaline pumped through my veins.

The couch dipped as he stood, and he shifted behind me. When his big hands cupped my ass and flexed gently, I swallowed hard and held my breath in anticipation.

"You are so fucking gorgeous." His voice was a harsh whisper against the shell of my ear. "You're all I can think about, and it's pretty fucking distracting." While he spoke, his hands slid over my arms gently. "Do you understand that you distract me at work? When I'm supposed to be focused? All I can think about is touching you again."

"Xander…"

He leaned forward and nipped my shoulder hard enough for me to yelp. "I feel out of control." Using his tongue, he laved the stinging injury. "I don't want to be out of control."

Not sure what to say, I whispered, "I—I'm sorry."

His voice was tight. "Are you? Or are you trying to break me?"

"What's happened? Are you…"

My voice trailed when he slid his hands up over my back, unsnapping the buttons along my spine in a swift motion. "I've been dying to do that since I dropped you off at rehearsal earlier. In the car, I considered ripping it off of you."

He sounded desperate, like he was barely hanging on to his control. "Y-you could have done that before we left."

"I should have. Then maybe I wouldn't feel like this."

Was there something I'd missed? Was something wrong? "How do you feel?"

His voice was soft, but I could tell he still spoke through clenched teeth. "Like I'll die if I don't touch you right now."

His hands trembled as they smoothed down my back, making me feel his desperation. "I'm yours."

2

XANDER

I stared down at her. Her strong back was bare now, and I could see the strength in her muscles. She'd straightened her hair today for rehearsal, and it hung thick and free. Her leggings-clad arse was upturned toward me. I wanted to bite it.

And spank it.

And Christ, I wanted to fuck it. Would she let me?

No. Not tonight. I needed her too much. Control wasn't even in my vocabulary right now. The fury was too close to the surface. Hell, I shouldn't touch her at all. I should have gone to Notting Hill, called Miriam or someone else from the service and worked out my frustration.

The problem was that I *only* wanted her. But I was on

a precipice between sanity and oblivion. I wanted to mark her in ways no one else had. Christ, I was losing it. She wasn't a whore. I couldn't treat her like one. I wasn't going back to that place. Not with her. She mattered. Tonight, I'd thought I was protecting her. When I thought Easton wanted to take her from me, I'd considered killing him. And I could have done it easily.

That was how much she owned me now. And she had no bloody idea.

I'd come straight home after leaving Lex's and tried to calm myself down. But everything I'd tried had just made me more keyed up. It alarmed me to realize that what I needed was her.

I needed her too damn much. And now here she was, offering herself up to me. My cock twitched painfully in my jeans, and I tried to rationalize with my inner demons. Telling them that they didn't want out. That this was a result of my fight with Easton. That what I wanted was to take care of Imani. That I didn't want to scare her off.

But the demons weren't listening. Shaking with anticipation, I looped my hands in the waistband of her leggings and yanked them down her legs.

Her gasp was sharp, but she didn't protest.

In the darkness, I could just make out the sweet lips of her pussy, and I wanted to bury myself inside her deep and never come up for air. Her scent surrounded me even as I fought for some measure of control. But it was no use around her.

With her knees apart, I helped her tug the leggings and her thong all the way off her legs.

When her legs were bare, I repositioned her so that her legs were parted, bracing her on the couch properly in the perfect position for me to slide home.

But as her scent wrapped around me, driving the need that took over my body, I knelt behind her. "So fucking pretty."

The first taste of her on my tongue was better than anything I could think of eating. She was sweet, spicy, and I lapped at her swollen lips like a starving man. *Please, God, please let me die like this. Let this be my final resting place.*

Her breathy moans spurred me on, and I spread her lips with my fingers, exploring every inch of her. Unable to leave any part of her unexplored. When I wrapped my lips over her clit, she moaned my name and scored her nails on the fabric of the couch. That's what I was looking for from her. Something deep and primal drove me on. I had to mark her as mine. I flicked my tongue against her clit, and she screamed. And when I slid a finger into her, pressing the raised flesh at the front of her tight, silken walls and stroking her G-spot, she came around me with a tight grip on my finger.

Watching her come, knowing I'd taken her there, should have calmed me a little, but it didn't. It just drove me harder. I wanted *more*. Wanted to make her beg to come again and again and again.

I kissed her inner thighs before standing behind her. I quickly shed my clothes and grabbed a condom out of my wallet. Her smooth, wet lips beckoned to me and I couldn't resist sliding the bare tip of my cock through her folds.

"Oh my God," she ground out.

When I aligned the tip to her sweet opening, I could still feel the tremors of her around the head of my cock. I stood perfectly still, letting her convulse around me, before I pulled back with a growl.

Shit. What was I doing? I'd never once had sex without protection. It didn't matter how good she felt. I didn't take risks like that. Sliding the condom on, I aligned myself back to her slick core.

Imani canted her hips backward, and I bit my bottom lip. *Go slow, go slow, go slow*. But I was too far gone to listen to my meddling brain. She was so wet, I slid in all the way with no resistance. Like she was made for me.

She gasped and dropped her head to the headrest as I drove into her again and again. Her inner walls stroked me, massaging steadily. My blood boiled, and I gritted my teeth against the impending orgasm, the feeling of freedom within reach. But it didn't come. Focusing all my attention on her and the sensation around my dick, I gripped her hips tighter, my fingers pressing into her honey-colored flesh.

The sweat dripped off my brow as I filled her, so high on the feeling of being inside her that I never wanted to be anywhere else.

But I was no closer to letting go. "Play with yourself. I want to feel you coming around my cock."

She obliged, and I pumped faster as she chanted my name. But even with each slide in to her warm, slick depths, I wasn't any closer to release. With a snarl, I released one hand and joined it to hers, sliding over her clit. I tried to rub faster, but she slowed me down. I tried to control it, but she intertwined our fingers, making me take my time.

When I yielded to her, the tingle started in my lower spine. *Fucking finally.* If I could just come, I could be rid of the fear that chased the adrenaline. I didn't want to keep thinking about what would have happened if she'd been on the barge tonight. The moment I lost focus, the orgasm that was so close evaporated into thin air.

But hers slammed into her. "Xander! God. Yes. Right. There. Yes, yes, yes."

I fisted a hand into her thick hair as I fucked her. "You like that." Need drove me in as far as she would take me. Her only answer was a low moan. "I know you want more. I'm not stopping until you come again and again around my cock."

Leaning forward, I nipped the back of her neck and kissed that spot just behind her ear. But it was no substitute for kissing her. For feeling her lips against mine. Her tongue tangling with my own.

Suddenly, she grabbed the back of the couch and stopped moving, locking her hips in place. Imani turned her head and brushed her hair off her shoulder. "Xander."

I didn't meet her gaze, and instead, kept looking straight ahead. I didn't want to see the concern in her eyes. I didn't want her to see the desperation in me. I wanted to avoid the intimacy. Wanted to hide the truth from her—that I needed her. I didn't want to, but I knew I craved her. I slid my fingers over her clit and reveled when she shuddered again. "Come for me."

She shook her head. "Stop."

The word was like a slap of ice-cold water, and I immediately stilled. "W-what?"

She moved her body forward away from me, and my hands tried desperately to hold her in place. "Xander, let me go." The sting of rejection had me stumbling back. But she reached out and took my hand. "Look at me."

I stubbornly refused, and I looked anywhere but at her. "It's okay. I'm going—"

"Xander." Her voice was firmer now, and I didn't want to see the worry on her face. But I couldn't deny her and slid my gaze to hers.

"What?"

She licked her bottom lip and I stared, mesmerized. "Look at me, please."

When I raised my gaze, I saw the heat I was accustomed to seeing. She wasn't rejecting me. Then why had she stopped?

She must have seen the question in my gaze because she tugged me closer and shifted her position until she lay back on the couch. I settled between her thighs, and my gaze slid down her body. I swallowed thickly, homing in on her wet lips where I wanted to bury myself again. "I don't understand."

Her smile was soft when she spoke. "A second ago, you weren't with me. Now you are."

All it took was her tongue sliding over mine, and the promise of bliss was back. I started to spiral out of control again, but in a good way. The emotional connection I'd been avoiding, that's what was missing.

Imani anchored me.

She took my hand and slid it to her breast, and I

relished the softness of her skin. "Imani," I breathed. She arched into my caress, seeking more of my touch.

The emotion welled so deep in my chest that I feared I might choke on it. God, she fit into my big palms perfectly when my thumb traced over a nipple. Her hips rose, bringing her slick sweetness sliding over my cock. I took full advantage, sliding home, seating myself fully inside her. When I stroked deep, she threw her head back, gasping my name.

With a heavy-lidded gaze, I watched her, the unabashed way she responded. And I knew in my bones that I was falling for her. The well of emotion spilled over the lightning starting up my spine. "Fuuuck me."

Before the white-hot flash of heat took me, she started to come around my cock again, her tiny convulsions gripping me. When she fisted her delicate hands in my hair and pulled me to her neck, my orgasm slammed through me. Unable to keep anything from her, I poured everything I had inside her.

I blinked away the stinging in my eyes and nuzzled her neck. I wasn't letting her go.

I had a few weeks until the gala. I could convince her to take me seriously, convince her to stay.

Whatever it took. I needed her too damned much to lose her.

XANDER

After grabbing a shower and getting dressed, I watched her sleep. It was definitely high on the creep-factor scale, but I wanted to be near her. Early morning sunlight streamed into the bedroom through the shades, lighting her softly.

I wanted to photograph her. With the sheet thrown over her body and her hair rumpled and curling in every conceivable direction, she looked content. And I liked that I was the one who'd made her that way. I also didn't feel as out of control as I thought I would. Being with her hadn't spun me out. Just the opposite. It had anchored me. Once I stopped fighting her, that was.

She stirred, and her lashes fluttered across her cheek as she cracked her lids open. She smiled when she saw me. "Morning," she mumbled.

Unable to resist, I leaned down and kissed her softly. She was so soft, like her lips were made for kissing. Especially for kissing me. "Morning, love. Are you hungry?"

Her stomach growled in response, and she ducked her head under the pillow. "I'm always hungry." She stretched her arms over her head, and the sheet covering her breasts slipped. Suddenly my mind was on a different kind of hunger altogether. But I beat back the urge to climb back into bed with her.

"Come on. I figured we could head to breakfast. Maybe call Lex and see if he and Abbie want to meet us."

She peeled her eyes open further and frowned. "You're dressed. Why are you dressed? How did I miss you getting out of bed?"

I laughed. "Well, you were out pretty hard if I do say so myself."

She threw a pillow at me and I ducked. "Smug bastard."

I nipped her shoulder. "Too right. And as soon as we're back from breakfast, I plan on putting you in a comatose state again. But first I need to feed my..." My voice trailed off as I looked for the right word.

She slowly sat up. "Not sure what to call me, huh?"

"Guess not. We've been playing house and you're posing as my fiancée, but that's different now."

She nodded slowly as she studied me. "I guess it is."

I wanted to say the word. *Mine*. But that was too much and would certainly scare her off. So instead, with a nervous laugh, I said, "Don't look at me. I haven't a clue how to do this. But I know staying away from you isn't really an option I'd like to explore any longer." *God, way to pussy out.*

She chewed her lip. "It's not like I have some kind of

manual either. I don't really— I mean I haven't really had a lot of relationships. And I don't really do the whole trusting-people thing, so this is hard."

Panic flared in my chest. I was fucking this up.

She didn't want this. I scrambled for a way to make sure she stayed in my life. Fuck. We'd start with the bed. We were good there. I could bring her around with great sex, right? "Why don't we just take it easy and see where the meandering road leads? Maybe we'll make a good team." Fuck. Why did I sound like a complete wanker?

She looked down at her hands before slanting me a glance. "Xander, you're paying me to be here. It doesn't feel… right."

Bollocks. I knew the money would come back to haunt me. "I already wired the rest of the money into your account this morning when I woke up." My heart hammered as I searched for the right words. Not too clingy but interested. *Yeah, more like desperate, mate.* "I want you to stay because you want to."

She frowned up at me. "Why did you do that? I could be the kind of person to walk out."

No. Please no. *Swagger, mate. Believe it.* I shook my head. "Because I'd like the real girlfriend instead of the fake one, if you don't mind. I mean, I'd like you to stay until I hear about the position on the board of the Trust, but even when you move back to your place, I'd like to see you. *A lot.* Exclusively." *Way to piss all over her, you knob.*

My stomach knotted as I watched her. What if she said no? Well, I'd give her so many orgasms she'd be too weak to say no. That sounded like a solid plan.

She bit her lip and blinked up at me with misty eyes. "I'd like that. Just one thing, though."

That knot loosened, flooding my body with enough emotion to make me shake. "Name it."

"Maybe it's time we start *talking* through some stuff? Last night was…"

Leave it to her to bring up the hard thing. I winced. "Believe me, I know how fucked up that was." I swallowed. "You're not a whore. I shouldn't have treated you like you were." The hot wash of shame splashed on my face before she put a hand on my arm, and I had to resist flinching.

"You didn't hurt me. And I didn't feel like a whore. Besides, some of my friends are whores."

How did she do that? Make me want to laugh even when things hung on the precipice of going horribly wrong. Through gritted teeth I muttered, "Fine. Not a whore then. But somehow, I guarantee if I check your inner thighs, I'll find some bruises. I wasn't gentle when we started." Or the two times I'd woken her up with my mouth on her clit and my fingers digging into her flesh. I'd almost forgotten a condom that second time too.

She sighed and gathered the sheet more tightly around her. "I liked it. If you must know, I've got a sex hangover. I've got sore muscles I didn't know I had. And you're, uh, big. So yeah, I am a little achy, but I quite like the feeling. I can just imagine the state my hair is in right now."

My gaze scanned over her, cataloging everything about her from her slightly flushed cheeks to her heavy-lidded gaze and the beard burn on her shoulder. And her hair was in a tangled bird's nest situation. I'd have to get some of those satin pillowcases she had in her bed for this room too.

"You're sure I didn't hurt you?"

She squeezed my bicep. "I'm sure, Xander."

"Okay." Nervously, I licked my lips. "So, you're saying the chances are good I could *not hurt* you again?"

She laughed and flopped the pillow over her eyes. "Hell yes, but you're going to have to feed me first. Because this woman cannot live on incredible sex alone."

"One massive English fry-up coming right up. But first, a kiss." I slid my lips over hers, and need slammed into me quick. But unlike the compulsions I couldn't control, the compulsion to destroy myself, this felt good.

It felt light, like sunshine. I broke the kiss before I wound up crawling back in bed with her. "Let's get you fed."

"And then more kissing?"

The relief was almost crippling. She was staying. I had more time to convince her to love me. I could do this. "You drive a hard bargain."

3

IMANI

All I heard when I answered the phone that morning was high-pitched squealing. The kind only my sister could make at a decibel that probably drove most dogs insane.

"Ebs, I'm gonna have to ask you to stop screaming. Use your words. I can't hear you."

"I got in. I got. In. I got in. I. GOT. IN." That was all I caught before the high-pitched yelling continued. Ebony was generally excitable by nature, so I had long since learned to just put the phone down until the squealing stopped. When it finally went quiet on the other end of the line, I picked the phone back up again.

"Awesome, you got in. Now, do you want to tell me what you got in to?"

There was more squealing, but somewhere in the mile-a-minute teenage chatter, I caught the word that meant the world to me. *Briarwood.*

I started squealing with my sister. Ebony had done her part. From her interviews to her test scores, she'd gotten in.

I danced around the living room laughing. "Oh my God, Ebs, you're going to love London. From the West End to the clubs in Brixton to the East End. There's so much culture and shopping and food. God, the food. And access to travel. You and I are going to be on a train at least once a month, just going somewhere different. This is great."

There was a momentary twinge of guilt when I thought of my father. He'd have no one to look after him. But I shook it off. I would still look after him the best I could, but Ebony was my priority. I'd promised my sister to come back for her, and now I could fulfill that promise.

"Oh my God. I am so proud of you."

"Thank you, Imani. I know I didn't exactly believe you when you said it was going to happen. I guess so much bad shit happened that I lost a little faith."

"I told you you'd get in. This is awesome."

Some of my sister's earlier enthusiasm waned.

"Except how am I going to pay for it? You had to come to the rescue and pay the mortgage. So Dad clearly isn't going to pay for it."

"What was that you just said about a little faith? I promised you if you got in I'd find a way for you to go, and I will." Briarwood offered scholarships, but not for boarding. Families had to deal with the money of either boarding accommodations or alternatives all on their own. So I'd need a bigger place for us to live. But with the scholarship, I'd be able to manage tuition... maybe. Things would be a little tight, but there was no way I was telling Ebony she couldn't go. Besides, with the money Xander had paid me, I'd have enough for the first term, buying me a little time to get the money for the next term. I could do this.

"All you have to do is pack."

"Are you serious?"

"Yeah, I'm serious. You're going to love London."

🍃🍃

XANDER

I took a swig of beer before settling down with my laptop. Though the moment I sat back, the lights flickered and told me someone was coming up the elevator.

When I opened the door, I was surprised to find Jean LeClerc on the other side.

"Jean. How are you? I'm surprised to see you here." More like fucked, because the one time I needed her, Imani was at rehearsal.

"I'm sorry to just drop in, but I was in the neighborhood on the way to meet Charlotte, and I thought you wouldn't mind."

"Of course not, come on in."

Jean nodded, and I thanked God; Imani had a tendency to spread out when she was working on part of the script. She'd left some things in the kitchen and living room. It would be hard to mistake that she was at least a frequent visitor.

"Would you like something to drink? I can open a bottle of wine."

The old man held up a hand. "No, no. Charlotte is waiting for me, honestly." He glanced around. "I like what you've done with the place. I haven't seen it since you had that artist retrospective five years ago."

My agent had suggested I go intimate instead of using a gallery, and he'd chosen my place for the event. The idea had made me a bit cagey, people riffling through my things and favorite pieces, but then I'd realized I kept nothing personal of myself in this place, so it wouldn't matter. It had been a huge success, and I'd sold every single piece that night. All save one. The one I kept in my bedroom.

"Oh yes, I remember you bought this modern piece I did with Amber Hruk. The Danish model."

"It was stunning." Jean shifted on his feet. "Listen, I just wanted to give you the news myself. The board has decided to accept you."

About bloody time. I was starting to think I was torturing myself for nothing. Over my racing heart, I could just hear another domino fall. "That's brilliant. Thank you."

LeClerc nodded. "You deserve it. I will tell you though, I am concerned about the fervor of discontent between you and Alistair McMahon. Alistair threatened to quit if we accepted you."

My lips flattened. The end would be the same, but it would certainly rob me of my satisfaction in seeing the fucker twist in the wind. "It's a shame. But I assure you, I harbor no ill will against Alistair, and I can be a professional." *Right up until I bury the twat.*

"I'm glad to hear that." He glanced around. "Where is that charming fiancée of yours?" His gaze landed on a scarf.

"She's actually at rehearsal. She'll be back—"

As if on cue, Imani walked in with her usual chirping. "Xander, please tell me you ordered food, because I am absolutely starving and if I have to wait for the delivery —" She rounded the corner and halted mid-breath. "Jean." She blinked as she tried to recover her composure. "How lovely it is to see you."

He gave her a beaming smile. "I was just asking about you."

I only half heard their exchange. My gaze never left her body as she came over, wrapped her arm around my waist, then kissed me on the lips softly.

I knew it. I was done. I needed her. But for more than the combustion that kept the sheets on fire. And she could slip out of my fingers now.

"Sweetheart, Jean just came to give me the good news. I've been accepted onto the board."

For a second, I convinced myself that a shadow crossed her beautiful features, but it was instantly replaced by a sunny smile. "That's fantastic news."

Jean nodded. "I also wanted to invite the two of you to our spring gala. It's a donor event and you'd be a guest, so no work for you. But it might be fun, and the board will all be in attendance. It's on Saturday evening. And then we'll formally sign you in on Tuesday after the bank holiday."

I glanced down at Imani and held her tight. We'd

come to an arrangement already. She'd said she wanted me. But I had no guarantee. If we didn't have this, there was nothing binding us. She could still decide I was more trouble than I was worth. I had six days to convince her to stay. I had my work cut out for me. "We will be there."

4

IMANI

"Imani?" Xander called from the other room.

"Yeah, Xander?" I jogged out into the living room only partially dressed for the gala. I had my dress on, but I hadn't had a chance to do anything with my hair or makeup yet. "What's the problem?"

He held up the loan application I'd picked up from the bank the previous afternoon. "What the hell is this?"

"Oh, uh, just paperwork for a loan. Ebony called, and she got into Briarwood Academy. So I can finally bring her over with me."

He waved the papers again. "Still doesn't explain these." His brows were drawn and his lips thin.

Why was he so mad? "Well, okay. Briarwood costs a lot of money. Like ten thousand pounds a year. My dad clearly isn't going to pay for it if he can't seem to stay on top of his mortgage payments, so I'm going to get a loan to cover what her scholarship won't. What's the big deal?"

"The big deal is you didn't *bother* talking to me about it. So much for wanting to talk more. I'll give you the money. If you won't accept, consider it a bonus for how well things have gone with LeClerc."

My stomach twisted. "Please recall our earlier conversation about how I'm *not* a whore. You can't just wave a magic money wand at me. Not now. Things are supposed to be different now."

His frown deepened. "Things *are* different now, so I can take care of you. I can give you money. I have a lot of it. Why won't you take it? How is this at all different than me paying you to pose as my girlfriend?"

And there it was, the white elephant I'd thought I'd been masking with the living room cushions. I could call it whatever I wanted, but I was still being paid to be there in a way. It didn't matter that we'd slept together. It didn't matter that he said he wanted to be with me. Fundamentally, he thought he could buy me.

"It just is. You were paying me for a specific job. One that's over after this weekend. I'm grateful for it, but I can't go back and tap the source because I'm short on cash. In case you haven't noticed, Mr. Buffett, I like to do things on my own steam. I was desperate to pay the mortgage. That was the only reason I came to the bank of Xander. I'm not desperate now. I have a way out."

He ran both hands through his hair. "Woman, why are you so fucking stubborn? I don't want you to be beholden to me. I just want to help."

"But it comes with strings. Think about how I feel about it, Xander. Fe offered to help out with the mortgage. I could have taken his money. But he's my best friend and I know that while he has plenty of it, it's blood money, so I wouldn't. It's not who I am. I fix things myself."

"That's ridiculous, Imani. You want your sister here. I can make that happen. Shit. I should have just brought her here already."

"I think you're forgetting that I move out on Tuesday, Xander. We go back to our normal lives. Sure, we're trying to… I don't know… date or whatever, but I can't take your money. That's not how it works. You can take me to dinner, but you cannot just give me thousands of pounds for my sister's tuition." Not to mention I thought we were past that now. That was what I got for starting to buy into the illusion.

He sighed. "It's only money."

It was never just money. "No. It's not. It's so much more than that." It was also about control and how I needed to have it over my life. There was no way I was going to be dependent on anybody, let alone Xander. "Now if you'll give me another thirty minutes, I'll be ready to go."

His frown deepened. "So, you're done talking about this? What if I'm not done?"

"Too bad, because we're going to be late."

He cocked his head, and the intense, focused glare he gave me sent shivers down my spine. "And if I say we're not going?" His gaze narrowed as he took in the low-cut dip of my dress and the mile-high slit up my thigh. "I could *convince* you to take the money from me."

The flicker of hope that we might be able to pull this off dimmed a little. Knowing his skills, he probably could coerce me into taking it. But he was doing it again. If I let him, he would use sex to try to control me. It was entirely different than Ryan, but it was still control. He could try to make me do what he wanted. He would make it all about my pleasure, of course. But I knew what it was about for him. He wasn't getting his way, so he would seek to use the only tools he thought he had in his arsenal. Sex and money.

Whenever we had even the mildest disagreement, he used sex to resolve it. Or at the very least to put it on hold temporarily. And he was trying to do that now.

"I've been looking forward to this thing for days. I've got the fancy dress on. I'm going."

"We're not done talking about this."

I shrugged and turned away from him. "If you say so."

⚜

Xander

I kissed her shoulder and she shivered. Would I ever get used to touching her? The more I did it, the more I wanted to. *Then fix your bloody fight.*

"You know, you're making it very hard to think, Xander." Her voice was soft, but even after an hour at the gala, she was still miffed with me, and I hadn't been able to shake our argument either.

My chuckle was low. "Well, that's sort of the point. I'm trying to get you to leave early so we can finish our conversation." So I could get her into bed and make her take my money. But something told me that was the wrong answer. Or at least not the one *she* was looking for to the money question. "These benefit dinners are torturously boring." I still felt on edge. Like somehow, I'd let more of her slip through my fingers. If we could just be close, I'd know we were okay.

Or you need to grow a pair and talk to her about how you feel.

I didn't have much time if I wanted her to want to

stay. If she left this week, it would make everything that much more difficult. I just wanted her to share things with me. And it seemed like all she wanted was to be on her own.

She sighed in my hold. "Remember, you're supposed to care about these things. You're about to be named to the board."

"I care about the outcome." *Ruining Alistair.* "The actual part of the donor glad-handing, I can do without. Besides, my fiancée looks absolutely amazing right now, and I can't seem to keep my hands off of her." *Fake fiancée,* I reminded myself.

She turned in my hold even as she rolled her eyes. "We're supposed to mingle at these things, right? Why don't you introduce me to some people?"

"Or how about we go home?" I lowered my voice so only she could hear me. "You slide off those shoes and brace yourself against the countertop with your hands. I could lift your dress and slide into you, hot and deep. Make you call my name, over and over and over again."

Her skin flushed. "Xander."

"What?" I blinked at her innocently. "What did I say?" Why wasn't she as on edge as I was? Didn't she feel the tension between us? Why wasn't she eager to fix it?

"You know, Miriam had it wrong. You're definitely a dirty talker."

I grabbed two champagne flutes and led us toward the balcony, but a striking brunette glided in front of us before we could make it. Every cell in my body seized. *Christie.*

She didn't even look in Imani's direction, just kept her eyes glued to me. "Hello, stranger."

I removed my hand from Imani's lower back. I didn't need to transfer any of my anger to her. But I felt the loss of her heat immediately. I wanted to keep her close, but I didn't trust myself. "Hello, Christie."

She deliberately ignored Imani, and it ticked me off. "Have you met my fiancée, Imani Brooks?" I couldn't lie to myself and say I didn't enjoy the pain I read across her face just a little.

Her face fell when she slid her gaze to Imani. "A pleasure. Congratulations on the engagement. I know Xander is a hard one to pin down."

Imani held her own. With a tilted chin, she said, "Well, I guess that hasn't been my experience. Everything has been a bit of a whirlwind romance, you know."

Christie's brows rose, then she narrowed her gaze and examined Imani closer. I knew the moment she saw the ring. She should recognize it. After all, it had been hers. She was supposed to wear it forever and never take it off. But a few words from Alistair and that had been the end of that.

"Imani, would you mind terribly if I borrowed Xander for a moment? There is something I need to speak with him about."

Say no. Say no. But ever independent, Imani just said, "Take your time."

I couldn't read her hooded expression, but I could feel her pulling away, feel the distance between us.

I wanted to go after her retreating form, but I knew I had to deal with Christie first. "What do you want?"

"She's a little young, isn't she?"

"Easy, Christie, you really don't want to go there."

"Sorry. I'd heard you were engaged and didn't believe it. I wanted to talk to you. Maybe apologize for how things ended."

"Oh, really?" Was it bad form to make the bitch beg? "You mean the part about where you walked out on me without giving me any chance to explain?"

She slid her gaze around. "Can we go somewhere? You know, and talk?"

"No. We can't."

She sighed. "Fair enough. I don't have enough words to tell you how sorry I am. I should have listened to you. Stayed. Worked it out. But the truth was, what Alistair told me, it was an excuse. A reason to leave."

"You're shitting me right now."

"You were always so secretive. Closed off. You

wouldn't talk about your past at all. You never opened up, Xander. I felt like I was dealing with a shadow of you most of the time. The only time I saw any real version of you was in bed."

"You could have done a number of other things besides walk out. You could have told me how you felt. You could have tried to talk to me. You could have even told me the real reason then. Anything."

She shook her head, her dark hair curling around her shoulders. "I've always regretted it."

I drained my champagne glass. "Are you done?"

Her already alabaster skin went deathly pale. "All I wanted to do was say I'm sorry. You didn't deserve that."

"Good thing for me, I already figured that out." I grabbed two more glasses of champagne off a passing waiter's tray. I downed them in quick succession.

She pursed her lips. "Look, I'm going to offer you a piece of advice that you can take or leave. The infant you're going to marry— maybe try being more open with her than you were with me. Share yourself. Don't keep her at arm's length. And maybe she'll never take off my ring."

I noted her shimmering eyes as she took the hallway to the left. But I had zero urge to go after her. The emotions warred inside me— anger, self-loathing, confusion, need, loneliness. They almost paralyzed me. But then I caught a glimpse of Imani at the bar. She said something, and the bartender erupted in a booming laugh as I shook my head.

No doubt she'd said something sassy. A smile tugged at my lips despite the turn my conversation with Christie had taken.

I *needed* Imani. It was more than needing to make my plan work. It was more than the sex. It was so many things. I needed her to laugh, to tell me off, to walk around the house in her socks saying lines out loud. *In my bed.*

I'd grown used to our connection. I'd come to need it for my basic survival. I wasn't letting it go. Not now.

I strode over to the bar, leaving my empty glasses on the counter. Standing directly behind her, I leaned down and whispered, "Come with me."

She tilted her head up and raised a delicately arched brow. "I was busy talking to Sean here. He knows where I'm from."

I could give two fucks about Sean. And the git needed to keep his grubby paws off of her. To Sean, I lifted a brow. "Piss off, Sean."

She shook her head. "Sorry. He's a mite possessive."

"Too fucking right," I muttered, glaring at the knob who was busy staring at Imani's cleavage. I leaned in right next to her ear and said, "You left me back there."

There was mischief in her eyes but also pain. I'd hurt her. "It looked important. I know how private you are, so I left you to it."

A prick of awareness pierced my need. Did I treat her the same way I'd treated Christie? Or was this about her and her tendency to pull back before she had to care about anything?

"I'm sorry about that. I'll tell you anything you want to know. But first I need to taste you. To have you melting on my tongue... I need you."

Her lips parted, and for a moment I was worried she'd tell me to fuck off. But instead she nodded and took my hand with barely a muttered goodbye to Sean. I had no idea where I was going, as I wasn't familiar with the venue, but a map posted in the hallway told me exactly where I needed to go. The farther we got away from the crowd, the more I needed her, the more I craved her.

When I found the study located on the second floor, I tugged her inside and locked the door behind us.

"Xander, what's going on?"

The words tripped off my tongue before I could stop them. "I need you. *Now.*"

Imani's eyes narrowed. "What's wrong? What did she say to you? Swear to God, I will kill her."

The swell of pride in my chest eased my desperation

some. She might be angry with me, but she was willing to fight for me if I wanted. "Nothing important. I just need you."

Her gaze searched mine. "Okay, then. Talk to me."

I wasn't in the mood to talk. "Fuck now. Talk later." Before she could argue, I kissed her deep. Those pulling, drugging kisses I knew she liked. She made a little squeaking sound at the back of her throat, and I forced myself to gentle my touch. To take it slower. To not push so hard. But the need coursed through my veins, and I shook with it. The tension coiled me into a tight string, ready to snap at any moment.

I expected her to push me away. To tell me I was too intense, too much. But she sighed and slipped her hands into my hair, and I knew she wanted me too. Backing her up against a chaise, I leaned over her. "Sit."

"What?" She blinked up at me in confusion.

"You heard me. Sit."

She did as instructed. "Now hands on the back of the couch. Hold on tight. I don't want you letting go."

She blinked up at me with heavy-lidded eyes. "Okay."

The red dress hugged each of her curves. Her tits had been teasing me all night, swelling over the fabric, but never enough to be easy access, just enough to tease, to taunt.

"Open your legs, sweetheart."

"Xander?"

I dropped my voice. "Open. Now."

Slowly she slid them apart, the slit of her dress making way, giving her some room.

I kneeled in front of her and shoved aside the fabric. "All night I've been wondering if you were wearing panties. Are you?"

She cocked her head. "Why don't you find out for yourself?"

Shoving away the fabric, I tugged up part of the bodice to give her legs more room.

Fuck. Her scent surrounded me. Intoxicating me. I was buzzing from the combination of alcohol, need, and her. Mostly her. Because I knew even if we were at home, I would feel the same way. I'd still want her this badly.

I pushed her legs apart, and she whimpered. "That's it, baby. I want to see how pretty you are." And God, she was beautiful.

She'd waxed for me. And her honey-brown skin gave way to swollen lips that I wanted to taste. Merely a breath away from the promised land. When I parted her flesh with my thumbs, she trembled. "Don't forget to hold on, beautiful. I'm going to take my time until you melt."

Just the promise of pleasure and she raised her hips in invitation. I locked my jaw. I wanted her so fucking bad.

I slid my tongue over her lips, and she immediately cried out. Sweet, spicy and so good. I licked at her again and again.

Imani grasped onto the couch and raised her hips, begging me silently to keep loving her.

And then, as I held her legs wide with my hands, I fucked her with my tongue. She screamed and forgot all about holding on to the back of the couch. Her hands slid into my hair, holding me to her. Her essence practically dripping down my chin.

"Xander?" Her voice was shaky and raw.

"Just trust me, Imani." I sipped at her lips again. "Can you trust me?" I knew she had problems with trust. Problems opening up. So did I, but I wanted to show her that I would take care of her.

"Y-yes," she whispered hoarsely.

With a grunt, I grabbed her ass and lifted her more to me, spreading her cheeks slightly. I licked at her forbidden hole and made love to the tight pucker. Licking and pleasuring her while my thumb pressed hard on her clit.

Her breathing went choppy, and I loved the desperate gasps she took as she ground her hips into my face, begging me not to stop. With my thumb on her clit, I slid a finger deep inside her and curved it until the pad of my finger rubbed over her G-spot.

Imani blew apart, her body convulsing as the orgasm hit her hard. *Yes. Fuck yes.* I loved nothing more than watching her come.

As her body convulsed, I drew back with a growl and flipped her over onto her stomach. Her limbs moved easily as I positioned her. I slipped on a condom quickly, then, in one swift stroke, I slid into her to the hilt. "Fuck. So fucking good."

5

IMANI

Xander shook behind me, and I panted as the aftershocks from my orgasm pulsed around his hard length. He was so big. But it felt so good as he rubbed against my G-spot.

He kissed my neck and nipped it gently as he reached under me and cupped my breast. With the slightest movement of his hips, he sent shockwaves through my body.

"I love you in this position, that perfect ass of yours offered to me as if on a platter."

"Xander." Deep down, I had sensed this part of him. The darker him. The unrestrained him. I'd seen flashes of it before, but he'd tempered it for me. Like he didn't want to hurt me. I didn't want it tempered. I'd been holding back my whole life. Now was not the time to do that. I wanted to feel alive. I liked how I felt in his arms. Possessed. Like this was where I belonged. "More."

His hips picked up speed, and the edges of my vision grayed. "Yes. God. Like that," I moaned.

"You like it when I fuck you deep?" His whispers were harsh against my ear. His breath hot. "You're so fucking beautiful. So perfect."

I was close again. His grasp on my breast tightened, and I knew oblivion was seconds away. He dug his free hand into my hair and tugged until I turned my head, exposing the skin just behind my ear. His favorite part to kiss.

"God, your pussy is so fucking tight."

I cried out when he started to pull out of my body. I turned so I could meet his gaze. When only the tip of him remained inside, he stroked back in. Our eyes locked.

His gaze held me captive, and I didn't dare let go. Through clenched teeth, he whispered, "You fucking own me. Body and soul."

Sliding a hand down my belly, all it took was the mere brush of his finger and I flew apart again, clamping down around him.

Four more pumps and Xander shouted his release, his cock kicking deep inside me.

Even in my boneless, exhausted state, I knew we'd

crossed some kind of invisible threshold. I only wished I knew what it was.

⸻

XANDER

Everything had fundamentally shifted for me. It was one thing to try and protect Imani from me. It was another thing entirely to try and protect myself from Imani.

Last night, what happened to me, was impossible to run from.

Arrangement or no arrangement, I knew I wasn't ever going to feel like that again.

Newsflash, first time you let yourself feel in a long time.

I rushed home to try and see her only to find the flat empty. When I checked the calendar, I realized she wasn't due home from rehearsal for another two hours.

Why the hell hadn't I double-checked? I would have just gone to the theater and watched her rehearse and maybe reminded her costar to keep his hands off her.

I could head to the theater to catch the rest of her rehearsal. Maybe we'd do dinner.

Smother much?

I needed to be careful not to overdo this. It had been

some while since I had been in an actual relationship, and I had no idea how to do this properly.

If this *was* an actual relationship. I was *paying* her to be here. If I wasn't, would she choose to be? Trying to guess wasn't going to solve anything.

I headed toward the bedroom to take a shower and noticed a box with Imani's things sitting by her door. What the fuck?

Easy does it. You knew shit would end eventually.

I knew this feeling. Like someone was slicing me open. Reaching for my guts. Destroying me.

Maybe she was just prepping to go, trying to make her departure as less fussy and messy as possible.

Our arrangement had been predicated on temporarily needing to look respectable with her while I dealt with the Alistair thing. And we were nearing that conclusion. I'd always known that she would inevitably go home. It wasn't like this was some kind of girlfriend experience; she wasn't an escort, and she'd been trying to tell me that from the beginning.

But last night… Last night a line had been crossed. One I didn't know how to go back from. One I didn't *want* to go back from.

I wasn't going to let her go. She was going to have to stay.

For what reason? You don't actually need her anymore.

Yes, I did. She was mine. And I would be forever broken if she walked out the door.

So keep her.

Two hours later, when she walked through the door, I was waiting on the couch with the lights dimmed low and the television on.

She gave me a wide smile after she dropped off her bag. "What are you doing in the dark?"

"It's not dark. Just consider it mood lighting."

This was going to be hard, but I couldn't pussy out. I reached for her. "Come here for a sec."

With a sexy smile, she toed off her shoes before she sauntered over. When she joined me, I took her hand and pulled her into my lap before kissing her softly. She tasted so sweet. All I wanted to do was revel in the feeling, hold onto her forever, but I knew I couldn't *tell* her to stay. I had to ask.

Look at you, learning the right way to do things.

"What's with you, Xander? You seem off."

I gently tucked her hair behind her ear. "I found your box."

She frowned and pulled back to meet my gaze before sighing. "Oh." She cleared her throat. "I'm not leaving today or anything. I know we've got a few more days, but I figured I should probably start to depersonalize the flat as much as possible."

53

"Is there a reason you're doing it right now?"

She squirmed on my lap. "Your *coup de gras* is coming, right? I don't want to have to do some long process of taking stuff out of here. You have a life you want to get back to. You said we'd see each other, and I want to. Do you really want this to be drawn out?"

"How can you ask me that question after last night?"

"I know that we said that we'd still see each other, but you realize we did this all backward, right? We moved in together before we even knew each other, and now things are different. We probably want to start fresh, you know?"

I shook my head. "I don't want to start fresh."

She laughed. "Really?"

"What I am saying is that I don't want to start over. I want you to stay. I don't want you to move out."

"I'm..." She paused.

"What?" *Just be brave you wanker. For once.* "Look, I don't know what any of this means. Obviously, it would be better if things were simpler, but I don't want you to move out."

What I really wanted to do was club her over the head, drag her to my room and chain her to the bed, and then spend the next several hours with my mouth on her pussy until she begged for mercy and agreed to never leave me.

But that was a scenario for another day. I knew she needed the asking part.

"Xander. That's a really big step, and this is already complicated enough. I'm not sure that that's a good idea."

"It's the only good idea. Are you happy?"

She ducked her head. I slipped my finger under her chin and lifted it so that our gazes met. "Are you happy with me?"

She nodded "Yeah. But Xander, we both have all this shit and things going on, and it's very complicated. When I'm here, I *believe* this. Us."

"And when you're here I believe it too. So maybe we make it real. At least stay for another few weeks. After the show's over and things are done with Alistair, we can have a moment to see what we're doing, where this is going."

She frowned at me then. "You're serious?"

I nodded. "Yes, I'm being serious."

"Wow. I didn't expect this. It's more than sex for me, Xander."

How could she not know? "It's far more than sex for me, too. If you leave here, you're going to strip my soul bare, and I'm not sure I can survive that. There's just still so much we need to learn about each other, and I'd rather do that with you here. A few weeks is all I'm asking for. If you still want to go after that, fair enough."

Yeah, not fair enough. I would be keeping her in my bed so she wouldn't leave me, but better to let her believe she had a choice in the matter.

"You really want me to stay?" Her brow furrowed.

"Isn't that obvious?" I ran a hand over my face. "I've never done this before. Or felt like this. I mean, yeah sure, I was almost engaged once for like a minute, but it wasn't like this. No one ever called me on my shit, made me see myself, made me let them in. I don't want to lose that."

Her gaze searched mine. "Okay, I'll stay. But only for a few weeks and then we'll re-evaluate."

"Yeah. I'm just asking for a few weeks. I just want a little bit more time. After that, if you want to go, I won't try to stop you. But we have something special here, and I want to explore it."

She nodded at that. "I suppose this is the part where you kiss me and we shag like rabbits on the couch?"

I clutched my chest and swore. "My God, I'm an animal, but I'm not a bore. I'm going to drag you to the floor, tear your clothes from you, and then dick you so good you forget your name."

She giggled. "God, you say the sweetest things."

I nodded "Yeah, I do, don't I?" And then I slid my lips over hers.

I'd bought myself some more time. All I had to do

was concentrate on showing her just how good it could be.

I was going to be the perfect boyfriend. And then a couple of weeks would turn into a couple of months, and before she knew it, she wouldn't want to leave. I could do that. She was mine. I just had to convince her. That's all.

"**B**itch, start talking."

Fe sat back on his couch with his arms crossed and a scowl on his face.

I sat across from him and sipped my tea. "I know you're ticked off."

"You don't even know the definition of ticked off. Do you understand that I had to find out about my bestie's relationship with *royalty* from *OK*-freaking-*Magazine*? I mean, without so much as a heads-up from my best girl. What the fuck, Imani?"

"Fe, I'm so sorry. You have every right to be upset. I should have told you. Or at least warned you about what was going on."

He sat forward. "Okay, so what exactly is going on? I turn my back for two seconds and fuck off to Ireland for work. Next thing I know, you're jetting off to Paris and dating the hottest photographer London has ever seen."

I smirked. "Okay, yeah, he's pretty fit."

"I am pea-green with envy. I swear you are such a cunt. This calls for alcohol."

I sighed. Where the hell did I even begin? "Okay, you have to promise me you're not going to freak out."

His brows snapped down. "When do I freak out?"

"Excuse me, do you remember the time the dry cleaner ruined your Prada sweater? You went insane. Or that time we were on Oxford Street and you swore up and down you saw Beyoncé in a car. We chased that car for ages, Fe."

His eyes bugged. "That was different. First of all, that was Queen Bey! And secondly, that was my favorite Prada. I can keep my cool."

"No judgment?"

Stretching out his arms, he laughed. "Honey, look at me. Besides, you've met my two boyfriends before Adam, right? I think I officially live in a glass house."

"Good point." I dragged in a breath then exhaled and told him everything, starting from when I called Miriam. Through it all, Fe sat and stared at me, nodding and wincing where appropriate.

When I finally finished, he sat back. For several long moments, he said nothing. Just stared at me. "So, you mean to tell me he hadn't had an orgasm in years? Is he for real?"

I winced. That part I hadn't exactly meant to blurt out, but I needed to know how I should handle it from a guy's perspective. "Yes, he's for real."

"And you have the magic touch?"

"Apparently."

"So you apparently have magic snatch. We need to bottle it and sell it by the millions."

"Fe, be serious. It's hot, but I'm not sure how I'm supposed to help him. I mean what if my magic snatch, as you put it, stops working? Does that mean that *we* stop working?"

He laughed as he dodged my poorly aimed pillow. "This shit would only happen to you."

Laughing so hard I snorted tea up my nose, I threw another pillow at him. "Oh, come on, no other wise words? Nothing to say? I could seriously use some advice here."

"Well, the first question is, how do you feel?"

I pursed my lips. "I was afraid you'd ask something like that."

"Well, it's a valid question. I know your history, so I have to ask how you're feeling. I know your no-relationship stance."

"It's not like it's a life choice, Fe. I've just been disappointed enough to know better."

"Well, from the sounds of it, he isn't Ryan. So maybe that's not a fair comparison."

I ducked my head. "I'm terrified, Fe. I don't believe in that one perfect person for everyone. How many times do I have to tell you, 'The One' is a mythical construct we've been taught to believe thanks to fairy tales... and Hallmark. He's not real. And Xander certainly isn't him. But I feel so good when I'm with him."

"I get it. You're a cynic. And in your position, I would be, too. You had a dud right out of the box. And he was rotten and rancid to the core. Xander might actually be that rare breed of reformed bad boy. And maybe you're reforming him."

"I promise you I'm not. Look, he's so secretive about his past, about what he's doing. I'm following someone blindly, and you know that's killing me."

"Well, everyone has a few secrets. It's not like you told him all about your sociopathic, whiny bitch of an ex…"

"Well, it's none of his business. And not his problem. I'm dealing with Ryan."

"And by dealing with, you mean going to rehearsals and trying to avoid him?"

I slumped. "Pretty much."

"Not going to fly. You have to report him. He's a twat. And I promise you were not the first one he hurt."

"What do you suggest I do? It's my word against his. And he's already worked an angle with Charles. I swear, I had one move and he beat me to it."

"You can't be alone with him, Imani."

"And I'm not. I've managed it so far. But I have no other choice. This is my dream, and I'm not letting him take it away from me. I make sure all conversations are public." At least since the incident in the courtyard I'd done that.

"That's not enough. I know I can't make you, and this has to be your choice. But he's taken too much of your life already. He can't take the joy out of your rehearsals too."

"I just want to forget him and move on. I have enough to deal with between the show, and my family, and now Xander. Ryan is the last person I have energy for."

"I just hate the way it affects you. You're so closed off to things that can make you happy, and you're solitary. You need to date and have fun. I just want you to be rid of that arsehole Ryan forever. You need to enjoy Xander Chase. Just do us a favor and tell me he's fantastic in the sack."

I shook my head. "Fe!"

"Oh, come on, give a boy a thrill."

"Fine, he's very good at dirty talk."

"Mmm, I do love a dirty talker. Lucky girl."

"Don't you go getting all attached. Sooner or later something will go wrong. Besides, I'm moving out."

He nodded at me the same way he always did when he wanted to say *If you say so, but I don't believe you.*

"I'm serious, Fe. This isn't a forever thing."

"Have you stopped to consider if it's like that for him?"

"This is Xander Chase, he doesn't want me long-term. He's not that kind of guy."

My friend shrugged. "All I'm saying is people can surprise you for the better sometimes. Especially when you have a magic snatch."

"Fe!"

He laughed and still dodged my much better-aimed pillow. As I filled him in on home and school, I realized how much I'd missed him. He'd been gone for two weeks. But it felt like a life span had gone by already. "God, I missed you."

"I missed you too. Now, next time, don't let me find out something in a gossip rag. Call me."

"I will. I promise."

"And for the record, darling, even though I prefer this outcome with the fabulous new man and the fantastic show, the other version would have been good too. You know, where I help you, and for once your stupid pride doesn't get in the way, and you say thank you."

I really did love him. "Yeah, I hear you."

⚜

XANDER

It felt different than I thought it would. I twirled around in my chair and stared out my new window overlooking Westminster Abbey. I was exactly where I wanted to be. On the board of the London Artistic Trust and owning enough shares to topple Trident Media. This was everything I'd wanted for years. Now all I had to do was find the proof I needed.

I cracked my neck, shutting out Lex's words. *Revenge is empty, Xan. You'll have to let it go at some point.* Well I wasn't letting it go. Step two was complete. Now on to step three, which was to isolate and terrify my opponent before completely destroying him.

"I see you've made yourself comfortable."

The sound of Alistair's voice from my door made adrenaline shoot through my veins. I turned to face my opponent and kicked my feet up on my desk. "I am comfortable, Alistair, thank you for asking after me."

"You won't last six months in this job before you're

64

bored and off to your next distraction. All I have to do is wait you out."

I tipped my lips up into a smile. "You're amusing, Alistair. But I promise you I will be here. You see, I'm not easily run off. I told you I would make you pay, and I will."

Alistair glared at me. "Wasn't fucking my wife enough?"

I puffed with a humorless laugh. "I promise you it was more a chore than anything else. You're quite welcome to her." Alistair's face morphed into a red, angry mask, but I kept my hands in my pockets. Just as well, too, because I knew I could kill him easily. And explaining the blood stains in my new office would be difficult.

The other man did lean forward a little. "How is what's her name? Christie? Oh, now wait, that was your *other* fiancée. What happened to that one? By all accounts she left you once she realized you were unstable and delusional and in need of psychiatric assistance. I mean, it must've been devastating for you. Is that why you're so hell-bent on destroying me? Because I told your bird who you really are? She was bound to find out in the end, Xander."

I smiled, my teeth locked together. "You're a twat."

"And you're a desperate wanker who has always

wanted what I had. You were desperate for attention when we were kids and you still are. No one believed you then, and no one will pay you any attention now with your temper tantrum. What is it exactly you think you'll do here? It's not like you'll get rid of me. I'm a long-standing fixture."

I narrowed my eyes, fury pouring though my veins. *Do not lose control. Do not let him control you.* He wouldn't be here for long. I just needed to make sure I had enough shares, then I could implement the last part of my plan. Until that point, I had to keep a level head.

"I'm here to do a job, Alistair. You're the one who's making it personal." I finally sat up. "I am going to end you. Plain and simple. And you will remember the day you could have helped me and chose not to."

As Alistair strode out of my office scowling, my phone rang.

"Garett, mate, tell me you've got something." I pinched the bridge of my nose as I stared out the window.

My investigator cleared his throat. "I'm still working on the flash drive. There's a lot on there."

"Look, the flash drive is secondary. What I want is any info you have on the trust."

"I'll need some time, but I'm digging. So far, there's nothing like what we were looking for. No history of harassment complaints. From what I have so far, it looks like he left the hands-on stuff for photo ops and that's it. But I'll keep looking."

My gut twisted. There had to be something I could use. There was no way Alistair was a boy scout. I was not wrong about this. "Have you found anything at all? We're sort of running against a clock here."

"There is something, but give me a day to make the figures work. It looks like your boy has been cooking books for the trust."

"You're shitting me."

"No. I'm not. It's negligible, and the money skimmed from accounts isn't enough that they would notice, but the only one looking at the accounts as a whole is Alistair, so he's probably been doing it for years."

"Any idea where the money is going?"

"That's the thing. It matches some information I pulled off the flash drive. He owes money to Pushka, part of the Russian mob."

I whistled low. I'd only heard about them in terms of the news and maybe some whispered gossip from Nick, Lex's friend. His father ran many of the seedier clubs in London, including strip clubs. No doubt he occasionally rubbed elbows with the Russian gangs. "That's some fucked-up trouble to court."

"Tell me about it. I'll have something definite to look at tomorrow."

"Thanks, mate."

"If there's something to find, I'll find it."

⚜

XANDER

"Xander, were you ever planning on telling me?"

Shit. I knew I'd regret answering the phone when I had so much work to do. "Mum, hi. Care to tell me how I've disappointed you this time?"

There was a beat of silence. "I wish you wouldn't say it like that. You're not a disappointment. I'm so proud of what you've accomplished."

Damn it. I rubbed my chest, hoping the feeling that lingered there would go away eventually. Ever since meeting Imani, a whole host of feelings had worked their way into creases of my soul that I'd never thought about before. "I'm sorry. I didn't mean that. Just a long day so far. What's the problem?"

"Were you going to tell me about your girlfriend? A friend of mine mentioned it at a game of squash, and I had no idea what to say to her."

Shit, bugger, fuck.

The goddamn *OK Magazine* photos. I'd meant to

give her a call for a heads-up, then, as with everything else, like me being completely unable to keep my hands off of Imani, I forgot. "Listen, I'm sorry you were blindsided. But it's not like that."

I wasn't sure how much I wanted to tell her. I wasn't in the mood for lectures, and I sure as hell didn't have the time for them.

"Then what's it like? The magazine said you'd been dating her secretly for months. If you have someone special, Xander, I just want to meet her, that's all. I want to know about your life. Meet who's in your life."

I gritted my teeth. Up until Imani, there was no one in my life I'd ever take around my mother. Mostly because they were all throwaways. Every last one of them. And class wasn't exactly one of my usual requirements. Hell, a brain didn't usually factor high on my list either. Come to think of it, I'd never given any consideration to the kind of woman I'd bring around my mother, ever.

"She's a... friend. She went with me to the interview in Paris."

"Oh, so she's *not* your girlfriend."

Wasn't that the million-dollar question?

We slept in the same bed. A place I intended to keep Imani as long as possible. But I knew from what she'd said that she didn't trust me to stick. Fuck, I didn't trust myself to stick. But I wanted to maybe be that guy. I just needed more time to convince her that I could be worth sticking for. If she was staying, she'd eventually meet my mother.

"It's complicated, Mum. She's—" What, I was going to talk to her about women now? "Different."

"Well, from those grainy photos, I could see she's certainly beautiful. She looks a lot like Abbie, actually."

I swallowed hard and dodged the question. "Yeah, she is. She's just a little hard to pin down sometimes." Before I knew it, the words flowed out easily. Who knew, maybe my mother could help me shed a little light. "She's complicated and funny. But there's a part of her she guards like a feral animal. Every time I get near it, she stabs back with something pointy and deadly."

"Well, women are mysterious creatures. But sweetheart—and please don't take this the wrong way—you have a bit of a reputation. She might be protecting herself so that you don't hurt her. Keeping you deliberately at arm's length."

That sounded about right. "How do I get her to stop? I don't like it."

Her laugh rang clear on the line. "You really don't know anything about love, do you?"

Lex had essentially said the same thing. "Apparently not."

"You can try being vulnerable and honest with her.

Guard her feelings like you would guard your own. If something terrifies her, you make sure she never has to face that fear alone. Don't do that thing where you swoop in to fix it or change it. She won't thank you for it."

Hadn't I tried that very thing? It hadn't earned me her favor. "And if she won't share what her dark and scaries are?"

"Then, my beloved, you try patience."

Patience. Now where the hell could I go to buy some of that?

7

XANDER

A slice of harsh light pierced the darkness of my bedroom, and I cowered under the bed. I'd taken to sleeping there because it was safer. Sometimes Silas would think I was sleeping in my brother's room and would leave me be. Or he would tire of looking for me in all the rooms of the house. Or even better, he worried about my mother finding me so he would leave me alone.

But tonight wasn't one of those nights. "Where are you, boy? I know you're in here. I already checked the security footage. I know you haven't left your room all night. Come on out. If you make me look for you, I'm going to hurt you." Silas had been drinking, and his words slurred together as the smell of port drew closer and closer.

Under the bed, I shivered and tried to make myself as

small as humanly possible. Go away, just go away, please God, just go away.

Silas pushed the door open farther, letting the room flood with light, and in the hallway, I could see Alistair.

The older teenager was quiet and mostly sullen, having no time for his future stepbrothers, but I hoped that maybe, just maybe he would help. Maybe he knew the kind of monster his father was.

From my vantage point, I willed Alistair to look at me, silently begging, pleading. I shifted slightly so my future brother could see me more clearly. But when our gazes locked, Alistair merely stared at me. I mouthed the words, Help me.

There was something in Alistair's eyes that flickered, and I took a deep breath, thinking he would get one of the nannies or call someone, anyone to come help me.

But instead, after what seemed like minutes merged into hours, Alistair walked in behind his father and closed the door behind them. Fear snaked up my spine. Large, meaty hands clamped around my ankles and tugged me out from under the bed.

I thrashed. A distant part of my mind knew I was still in the throes of a horrific nightmare, but the other part did not. I felt like I was suffocating, unable to get air as I choked.

"Xander. Wake up!"

That voice. Soft, feminine but insistent. Calming. My consciousness gravitated toward that voice. I would be safe if I could just get to it. If I could grasp it, someone would take care of me. Someone would love me. All I had to do was get there and I could escape my nightmare.

Someone pushed me hard on the shoulder and yanked me out of the horror. Sweat clung to my skin, matting my hair, and I scooted back on my king-size bed with the sheets tangled around my legs. I dragged in several deep breaths as I struggled for oxygen and took in my surroundings. The room was dark, save the moonlight from the massive window overlooking London. I was in my room. I had access to two exits. I was safe. I didn't need to be afraid. *You are safe.* No, not yet, the only way to be safe was with Alistair in a body bag.

At the foot of the bed sat a wide-eyed Imani. She'd wrapped a sheet around her and watched me warily.

My stomach rolled and I swallowed hard. I wouldn't be sick. Not in front of her. I wasn't going to lose control. Not like that.

I scrubbed a hand down my face and tried to get myself under control. Eventually, my breathing evened out, and I slid my glance in her direction. "You all right? Did I hurt you?"

Imani shook her head slowly. She'd tucked her hair into a ponytail, but several of the curls around her face were making an escape. "Xander, that was a hell of a nightmare."

I was quick to apologize. "I'm sorry. They're unpredictable." I scanned her body for signs of injury, even as my mind made its silent plea. *Please don't leave me.*

"I'm not hurt. I'm more worried that you hurt yourself."

"I'm fine." The response was automatic and tripped off my tongue because I'd been telling myself the same lie for years.

She nodded, even as her gaze slid to the faint bruises on my knuckles. "Just like you were the night you got those?"

I balled my hand up into a fist before rotating it so she couldn't see the bruising. "That was—" What could I say? The violence of the other night was probably triggering something inside me. We still hadn't talked about it really. I hadn't wanted to.

"Nothing, yeah, I know." Her eyes were sad. "I'm only trying to help. But I'm not sure I can if you won't talk to me. Tell me what's going on. I want to know how to help you."

I itched to touch her, to hold her and not let go. But there was no way I could form the words to tell her that I needed her.

"Should I call Lex? Somebody else?"

"No." It came out harsher than I intended. "I'm sorry. I just—I don't need anyone's help."

She shook her head. "Don't push me away." She reached her hand out to me, and all I wanted to do was reach out and take it. But if I did, I'd have to open the door. It would have to come out, and I didn't want her running. *She's going to leave if you don't tell her. Might as well cut yourself open and bleed.*

My body still vibrating, I reached for her outstretched hand and pulled her close. She kissed me softly. "I'm here if you need me. Just tell me what's happening, and we can deal with it."

"Okay, just let me get us some clothes. I'll never be able to get through it if you're naked." More like I wanted some shielding in case she ran from me. Standing awkwardly, I snagged two t-shirts and boxers from my bureau. When we'd both donned the clothes, I sat on the edge of my bed. Imani scooted over and sat next to me.

"When I was a kid, my parents divorced. I was about five or so when they got divorced the first time. Very small. Mum was pretty lonely. She's the one with the royal blood so she had her flurry of social obligations, but she was mostly lonely and obsessed with finding us the right kind of father figure. Dad's a bit of a twat."

She kept quiet but still reached out and took my hand in hers, offering me silent support.

"She finally found someone. Silas McMahon. On the outside he seemed to adore Mum. He was attentive and wanted to spend time with us. He had a son from a previous marriage, but he was older. A teenager, and Silas hadn't really been around for his childhood much, as he lived with his mother. It seemed like an instant happy family at first. The more Mum trusted him, the more she left him with us alone."

Next to me, I could feel her stop breathing as she tightly held my hand. I squeezed my eyes shut. I could do this. I could.

"Late at night, Silas used to sneak into my room and…" The bile rose in my throat and I forced myself to swallow it down. "He touched me. Told me I liked it. That it was my fault it was happening. That I made him do it. When I resisted, he beat me."

"Oh my God, Xander."

I sniffed. "He told me that if I told my mother, then he'd hurt her. I didn't find out until much later that he'd also been hurting Alexi. But he had a preference for blonds. Lex was too dark for him. I was really tow-headed as a child." I ran a hand through my now dark-as-sin locks.

"No one helped us. Mum was blissfully unaware, and I've never forgiven her for it. At the same time, I can't blame her. I was wild as a kid, even before Silas came into her life. Around him, I was quiet, withdrawn. She thought he just had a way with me." I snorted. "Little did she know."

"Someone must have known, tried to help you. You were just a baby."

"Alistair knew."

Her shocked gasp filled the silence. "*He* was the teenager?"

I nodded and ran a hand through my hair again. "There was one night when I was hiding under the bed. I could see Alistair outside in the hallway, and I begged him to help me. To call somebody, to do something."

"What did he do?"

"He came in and he—" My voice broke as the memory threatened to choke me. "He held me down for his father."

Imani stared at me, agog, her eyes wide with horror.

"One night when Mum had traveled, Lex stayed in my room with me. My little brother, protecting me. Can you imagine?"

"He loved you."

"Yeah, he did what I couldn't. Silas came for me that night, but Lex was there. You should have seen him. So small and so brave. At six years old, he told Silas that he was going to tell. That he was going to call the police and

Silas would go to jail forever. I thought the tosser was going to kill him."

"Oh my God."

"The whole time, Lex was shouting at me to run, and I did. I can still hear his little feet behind me. I ran past our stairwell, and I was desperately looking for a room that would lock where we could hide. Then all of a sudden, I didn't hear Lex's feet. Just a curse, then several loud thuds in a row. When I turned back to go for Lex, I found him at the top of the stairs. He'd pushed Silas down."

"Fuck."

I scrubbed a hand down my face. "He saved my life. My brother had done what I couldn't do. He might seem quiet and affable, but he's a wall of strength, that one."

"You're strong too, Xander. None of what happened was your fault."

I laughed mirthlessly. "Maybe not, but my choices were on me. I told my mum and everyone that I had pushed him down the stairs. Of course, my father started his PR campaign. I don't think he ever believed I'd done it. There was something so steely about Alexi back then. I refused to let them send him to some boarding school far away, though. He was six, for the love of God. Instead, I went. To Dexter Academy. It was for troubled children, but very exclusive. I had my fill of shrinks and therapy while I was there."

"Did any of it help?"

"Some. A little. Not enough." I rubbed my jaw. "The one good thing that came out of that place, was that it gave me an outlet. It's where I first picked up a camera."

"Xander, you still turned out great. You can't keep torturing yourself over something that happened when you were a little boy."

I laughed. "You think I'm great, do you?" I gestured at my body. "This is the result of Alexi saving me again. If you'd seen me five years ago, you wouldn't be so eager to hold my hand."

"Stop it, Xander."

"It's the truth. There wasn't a drug I wouldn't try, no reckless thing I wouldn't do. No dubious woman I wouldn't sleep with. Screw that. *Women*."

"What happened? Why did you spiral after all your therapy?"

"I met a girl at uni. Christie. She was beautiful. So smart. You know, the kind of girl who kept me on my toes. I was going to marry her. She seemed like the answer to my prayers. But then I had a chance meeting with a grown-up Alistair. Let's just say it didn't go well."

"I hate him," she whispered. Ice dripped from each

word, and there was a fierce sincerity inscribed in her eyes that told me she meant each one.

"I'd never forgotten that night. And I lost it. I threatened to kill him, to expose what he was, what he'd done. He took it all in stride. The next day I caught him coming out of Christie's flat. He'd told her about my past. That I'd killed his father. Dad had covered it all up, and as far as the public was concerned, Silas had fallen after a night of drinking. But Alistair knew at least my version of what happened. And he told Christie."

"Please tell me she believed you."

I shook my head, the pain too hard to relive. "No. She left me." I inhaled sharply. "That's when the spiral started. My anchor was gone, and I blew a fuse."

"Xander, you were hurting."

Fuck. Why was she being so understanding? I scrubbed my face, unsure of what to tell her, how to tell her. "My chance at normalcy was gone, and I lost myself in women. In sex. You said it yourself; it's how I fix problems. There were hundreds of women. Sometimes two or three or more at a time."

She blinked at me rapidly but didn't let go of my hand.

"I was pretty much a sex addict. But the kicker of it was, the more women I slept with, the more disconnected I became." Just saying the words made me feel ill. "It was like I was trying to prove that what happened to me didn't affect me. But it colored everything. My relationship with my mother, with Lex. The women I slept with. Eventually, even sleeping with those women got tedious."

I gave a mirthless chuckle. "The irony was, because of my name and this face, more women approached me. All kinds of women. I wanted them all. I had to prove something. But I couldn't bring myself to care about any of them. Eventually, I couldn't even come anymore. Sex had become this habit. A way to numb the gaping hole in my chest."

"Xander." Her voice was so soft, but I could hear the tears in it.

"I ran my nutter arse back to a doctor pronto, but it wasn't physiological; it was psychological. Of course, the doctor said I needed some serious time on a couch if I wanted to stop. Shit, at the time, I could be with two or three women a day. It didn't help that the world's most beautiful women surrounded me. All it took was a look of interest and I would fuck someone. I didn't care where. A dodgy alley, a car, by the wharf, the loo at a club. Hell, I've had women blow me at one of the VIP clubs before."

The whole time I spoke she didn't let go of my hand once, just gripped it tightly as if she was afraid I might bolt.

"At one point I wondered if maybe I was gay." I shook my head, disappointed with myself. "That was a disaster of a failed experiment. I couldn't get it up. But at least it answered a question, though I still couldn't get my rocks off with anyone. Sure, I could come on my own, but it wasn't the same. I'd leave women in bed then have to do something to relieve the pressure afterward unless I wanted a wicked case of blue balls. The relief I couldn't get with sex I numbed with drinking and party drugs. Fuck, I didn't even like being high. I was a fucking mess. Until one night three years ago, Lex dragged me out of some East London club by my scruff." I shook my head. "It was humiliating, but he wouldn't let me give up on myself. I really had no choice but to get myself together. What I was doing wasn't working."

"You were able to just walk away?"

"It wasn't always easy, but I started choosing the thing that felt good. Or rather the path where I didn't feel like an arse. The drugs were easy to stop. I never liked being high. It was harder to quit whoring around. But when I did, it stuck. Until recently, I hadn't slept with anyone for two years." I swallowed hard, not wanting to tell her about what I'd done. But I knew I had to. "I shifted my focus to revenge over the last couple of years. Lex said it would eat at me, but I didn't understand what he meant until I met you. I've only cared about making Alistair pay, and I've been willing to do anything to make that happen. That includes sleeping with his wife for information."

She went still, but she didn't let me go.

I pressed on, hoping I could just get it all out before she decided she was done. "I knew who she was, and I targeted her. I slept with her. I told myself it was for information, but a part of me knew it was just because I wanted to punish him. We'll just say it wasn't good for me. And then you pretty much changed everything."

Imani parted her lips, and I fought the urge to kiss her. "I don't understand. Why me?"

"I wish I understood it myself. All I know is that I felt this instant connection to you that first night. Like a part of you was as afraid as I was, but you were so strong. I wanted to touch you. I was *desperate* to kiss you. Just tasting you was enough to have me on the edge of an orgasm."

Imani frowned as she tried to understand properly. Sitting up straighter, she asked, "Then why do you try to block out that connection?"

Well, I'd already told her the truth. Might as well continue. "Because you scare the shit out of me." I finally told her about the night I got the bruises on my hand and how badly I'd beaten Easton when he attacked me at Lex's and I thought he had come for her. "That night, by the time I got home, I was a wreck. You weren't here, and it kept running through my head what I could have done to that guy. It terrified me that you make me lose control. I would have happily killed him with zero remorse. Having someone that close to me petrifies me."

She swallowed. "You were *different* when we..." she let her voice trail.

I nodded. "I needed you. But I wanted to distance myself from you emotionally. The moment I tried to do that, we didn't work."

She nodded then reached up to my face and cupped my cheek. "It changed when I kissed you?"

I nodded. "I can't seem to hold back from you."

She planted her hands on my shoulders and kissed me softly. "Then don't. I'm here for as long as you want me."

Little did she know that forever sounded pretty good to me.

8

XANDER

This was it.

Today was the day. I was finally putting all of this to rest. But I still couldn't shake the shadow of last night. Imani hadn't left me, and I'd held her till the sun came up, still unable to sleep, but feeling lighter than I had in months. It didn't stop the raw, exposed feeling though.

To Imani's credit, she'd acted completely normal this morning, complete with shower sex that blew my mind. And if I was honest with myself, I'd rather be locked in the house with her all day, but I had other commitments now. LeClerc wanted to meet later today about one of our campaigns. But before we discussed work, I'd be presenting the old man with all the information I'd dug up on Alistair. When it was over, the man wouldn't be allowed into the building. I'd wanted a public spectacle and shaming, but the work the trust did was genuine. I didn't want that tainted by Alistair.

Before I could focus on my future, I had to deal with my past. Garett had finally found something I could use, though it wasn't what I expected. After last night's stock purchases, I was finally ready. I'd thought I'd be more excited about it, but mostly I just wanted it over with. I was just so tired.

This morning, Lex and I had made our move. In the next five minutes, the announcement would go out to all the media outlets regarding the purchase and control of Trident Media Group. We'd also leaked it that Lex and I were behind the company that made the purchases. No point in making someone twist in the wind if they didn't know it was you.

A knock on the door made me sit up straight in preparation. "Come in."

Alistair pursed his lips as he shut the door behind him. "Let's get this over with, shall we? What did you want to see me about? We have work to do today, and I don't really have time to deal with your particular brand of whiny bullshit."

My lips tipped into a half smile. I waited for the rush of victory, some sense of accomplishment, but I was too tired. Too empty. I'd hated this man for twenty years. The pain he'd caused me was unspeakable. But at the same time, the anger had only affected *me*. Eaten *me* alive. Alistair was, for the most part, unaffected by it.

Yeah, well, that was about to change, and then he'd be done. After this I could spend some time with Imani, get to know her for real, figure out how to live without the need for revenge. "Have a seat, Alistair."

My once almost-brother shoved his hands in his pockets. "I prefer to stand."

"Fair enough." I rolled my shoulders. "Within the next few minutes, I expect you to resign from the London Artistic Trust. I don't want to ever see you again. Matter of fact, I'd like you to move away from London. I don't really have any say about that, but if I do see you anywhere in London, I will make it my personal agenda to destroy you."

Alistair stared at me for a long moment then laughed. "Have you been shooting the stuff your heroin-chic models love so much? I'm not going anywhere. Nor am I resigning from the Artistic Trust. It's a prestigious position, one I work hard for."

I thought I'd be angrier, but I felt nothing, but complete apathy. "You will resign, and I'll tell you why. Since I took my position, I've been doing a little digging. I figured if I looked closely enough, I'd find something to pin on you. Hell, I thought I'd find that you were a sick fuck like your father was. I expected complaints of inappropriate behavior, payoffs. And don't get me wrong, I'm going to continue to dig."

I drew in a deep breath before continuing. I'd waited so long for this moment. "But imagine my surprise when I found you've been skimming money from several discretionary accounts. And even better, you've been using the money to pay off gambling debts. I asked around, and seems you owe money to a nasty bunch of Russian mobsters called Pushka."

"You're full of shit. You don't have anything on me."

I smirked, starting to enjoy myself just a little. "If you say so. I can't imagine Pushka will be pleased when the money dries up. Have you thought about what you're going to do?"

"You have no proof."

Unfortunately, the evidence Garett had found was circumstantial. It wouldn't hold up in court, but I wasn't taking this to court. I was going to press Alistair's balls so hard he would beg to step down. "Is that what you're telling yourself?" I held up a thick file. "It's all here, thanks to a little help from Jillian, or is it Julia? I can never remember your wife's name."

It was only then that Alistair's eyes bugged out. The older man lunged for me, and I stood smoothly, shifting my weight onto the balls of my feet. I'd been ready for this for a long time.

"You're a twat."

I shrugged. "Yeah, probably. But at least I'm not a thief. I haven't taken anyone's youth or money."

"What do you want to hear? That I'm sorry for what my father did to you? That I was afraid of defying him? That I knew the pain you were going through? Fine. I'm sorry. I wish I could take it back."

Fury propelled me until I had Alistair's lapels in my hands. There was a distinct lack of sincerity to the apology that made my blood boil. But more than that, I hadn't forgotten how the man had tried to ruin my life. "You're bleeding sorry, you git? Your lies destroyed me. And now I'm going to destroy you." I released him and Alistair stumbled back, his fear palpable.

"You don't understand; Pushka will *kill* me."

I shook my head. "Not my problem. And I'm afraid there is more bad news. As we speak, Alexi and I now own fifty-five percent of Trident Media. Starting as soon as we can manage it, we'll be dismantling your holdings brick by brick—everything you and your father built or that you built with his money. I'm not going to rest until it lays in a pile of rubble at my feet."

Alistair blanched. "You're a fucking liar."

"You can feel free to call your lawyer. You should have

been getting frantic emails by now. Our lawyers made the move for takeover this morning."

Alistair frowned and yanked his phone out of his pocket. With one glance, he threw it down. "What the fuck do you think you've done? This is my family's company."

"Yes, yes, it is, which is precisely why I want it razed. You will not profit any more from your family name. It's time you pay for what you let your father do to me."

Alistair planted his hands on my desk. "If you do this, I'll tell everyone that you killed him. The world will know."

"Go ahead. You do that. Open up those old wounds and cover-ups. I'll expose your father for the nonce he was. And given what he did to me and how good he was at keeping secrets, I doubt I was the only one he hurt. We'll see how many more of his victims come forward."

"Fuck you," Alistair sputtered, rage etched over his features.

Though I smiled, I didn't feel how I'd anticipated. All I felt at the moment was empty. "You know, rationally, I can forgive you for that night. You were a teenager. Still a child. I could have let you walk away from that. What I can't let you walk away from are your actions as an adult. You deliberately ripped the woman I loved away from me to protect your past. You did that to me willfully and deliberately. For that alone, I could kill you. But I'll settle for your livelihood instead."

"I will kill you."

"You're welcome to try." I held up my bruised fists. "But the last bloke who thought he'd have a go ended up in the nick for his efforts. Care to take your chances?"

"You cannot do this."

"Oh, but I can. You *will* resign today if you want to walk away with any of your money. Otherwise, I will make it my personal agenda to strip you of any fortune you have left. I will tell everyone on the board what you helped do to me." I shook my head. "I have nothing to lose anymore. You think I care what people say about me? I don't give a fuck."

"You're a dead man. I will destroy you."

I rocked back onto my heels. "Too late for that. You maybe could have been a decent human being. And maybe you were a victim of what your father did once, but no more. You've made this particular bed. Now you have to lie in it. I expect to see that resignation letter in my inbox within the hour. I'm meeting with LeClerc then. If you haven't resigned, I'll tell him everything."

Red-faced and blustering, Alistair pointed a finger at me. "We are not finished. This isn't over. I will see you rot for this."

"That's where you're wrong. We are done. I've been

twisting in the wind for years. Now it's over. Get the hell out of my bloody office."

As I watched Alistair walk out, I felt some relief, but mostly I felt numb. It was done. I was finally done. I'd leave the dismantling of Trident Media to Annabel and the finance guys. But I had survived and won.

Then why don't you feel better?

My phone rang, dragging me out of my reverie. "Xander here."

"It's Jean."

"Hi, don't we have a meeting in an hour?"

"This won't wait."

Something in the older man's voice told me I'd inadvertently fucked something up. "What's the matter?"

"The model, Bobby Reynolds, is she a friend of yours?"

Something about the way the question was asked told me to tread lightly. "I know her work. But can't say that I know her."

"Interesting that you would say that. Because she certainly knows you. She's refused to work with you and has pulled her support of the trust."

"What?" My brain scanned my memory banks. There were so many women, all of them blending into one another. I had no recollection of her whatsoever. "This is fucked."

"You're telling me. Come down to my office. We'll need to work through it today and come up with another solution."

"Yeah, I'm on my way." When I hung up, I ran my hands through my hair. After that scene with Alistair, it wasn't over after all. My past was still reaching out to fuck with me. I checked the time and groaned. It was already four. There was no way I'd be getting out of there in time to meet Imani for dinner.

I sent her a quick text.

Xander*: Stuck at work. Going to be a late night. I'm sorry. Rain check?*

The reply was instant.

Imani: *Okay, I'll miss you.*

Two minutes later a photo message came through. It was one of the ones I'd taken of her with my phone and loaded onto my computer. Imani, on the bed, bare-faced, the sheet barely covering her nipples.

My cock twitched, and I groaned against the spike of need in my blood. My hands were shaking when I tapped out a reply.

Xander: *I swear, I'm hurrying home.*

She sent me a smiley face in return.

Imani: *You do that.*

9

IMANI

I rolled my shoulders. Between rehearsals ramping up and a problem with a campaign at work for Xander, I'd barely seen him all week. I missed him. I'd told him I'd stay for as long as he wanted me. Was he tired of me already?

God, that was some weak bullshit. I had a home to go to. I couldn't freak out because he was busy.

Focus on what's real. Reluctantly, I dragged my attention back to rehearsals.

"Imani, that was great. Let's take it from the top of that scene again. Ryan, remember to give her something to work with. Make me believe that you love her but you can't deal with seeing her as your equal. I want to believe. I need to feel it, otherwise your audience won't. And watch your lines in the middle there. I think you skipped around. Watch Imani for your cues."

As Charles went back to his seat, Ryan's handsome face creased into a frown. While I was on today and completely in my element, he seemed off, unfocused. All day he'd been flubbing lines and missing his cues.

When we turned to take our positions downstage, I leaned in. "Where are you today? The longer you're out of it, the longer we have to stay."

The muscle in his jaw ticked. "Are you seriously going to marry that photographer?"

I blinked. "What?"

"I saw it in *OK Magazine*. I thought he was kidding when I ran into you at Rooftop Gardens."

"What business of yours is it if it's true or not?" Was he high? That would account for his current level of crazy.

He spoke through clenched teeth. "Come on, Imani. You know how I feel about you."

The bile threatened as my skin crawled. What the fuck was he saying? "And I have been honest as to how *I* feel about you, Ryan. I would rather have my skin peeled off without the benefit of anesthesia than voluntarily be near you." I didn't bother to look at him as I settled on my mark. I could feel him staring at me, but I resolutely refused to look at him.

Eventually he got with the program, and the rest of rehearsal went smoother. Ryan was more focused and gave me someone to act against, so it made my life easier. But it was one of the longest rehearsals we'd had to date, and I was done.

As my luck would have it, just before Charles released us for the day, I saw Xander at the top of the auditorium.

Even if his beautiful features were masked by the darkness, the way he moved gave him away. Also, the freshmen tittering in the corner as they gawked at him were a pretty good indicator of who stood in the shadows.

When I finished and said goodbye to everyone but Ryan, I took my time climbing the stairs, letting my hips sway with each step.

By the time I reached him, a devilish smile played across his lips. "You do love to tease a bloke, don't you?"

"Was I teasing?" I cocked my head. "I wasn't aware of any teasing. I just walked up the stairs." God, I'd missed him so much. I was in dangerous territory of really needing him.

He gave me the devil's own grin. "If we're being honest, love, I'm not sure who had the better view, me or that tosser you call an ex."

I shrugged off the shadow that crawled through me at

the mention of Ryan. "If you like, I can give you the same walk later."

"Deal." His voice was light and he smiled at me, but it didn't reach his eyes.

"What's wrong?"

He frowned at that. "Who said anything was wrong? I came to see my talented fiancée. Is there a crime against that?"

There was that word again. *Fiancée.* When he said it, I couldn't help but start to pretend that it was real. We were together but certainly not getting married. The whole situation was dangerous territory. "I guess not. What do you want for dinner? I'm starving. I could tear up some curry right about now."

He rocked back on his heels. "Sure. Whatever you want."

"Okay, come on," I said as I took his hand. "You might as well tell me what's bugging you. Your being quiet weirds me out. I'm used to you either ordering me around or flirting. This whole quiet, subdued thing really isn't working for me."

We walked out of the auditorium, and he dragged me to the courtyard, which was nearly deserted. "I wanted to give you something."

"Okay?" Anxiety had my stomach knotting into a tight ball.

He pulled out an envelope from his pocket, handing it to me.

Carefully, I opened it, then scanned the scientific jargon and the words negative farther down the page. "What is this?"

Xander sighed heavily and shoved one hand in his pocket, the other one scrubbing down his face. "After everything I told you, I can only guess my history worries you a little. So, I went and got myself tested a couple of days ago. Clearly, I'm no virgin, but," he shrugged, "maybe this wipes my slate clean a little."

Warmth bloomed in my chest and spread through my body as the knot in my gut loosened. "I don't need you to be a virgin. Those skills of yours come in pretty handy."

The sexy grin was back. "Want to clarify which skills in particular you find useful?"

I shook my head. "Thank you for this."

He licked his lips. "We're sort of in new territory here. I haven't had a relationship in a long time."

I understood his hesitation, and I had some of my own. I wanted him too. But could I trust someone like him? Too handsome, too rich, with too many secrets. But he'd already proven he was a better man than Ryan. Maybe it was time to take a chance.

"I guess we start slow." I licked my lips nervously.

"But this is a beautiful gesture. And I guess I'll match it with one of my own and tell you I'm on the pill."

His pupils dilated, and he groaned. "You can't tell me something like that when we're in public. It makes me want to drag you off to the nearest semi-private room and sink into you bare."

My brow arched. "So much for going slow."

He leaned his head back. "You're right. I'm sorry. I can wait until we get home."

"Your restraint is remarkable."

Laughing, he slung an arm over my shoulder. "So, is this a bad time to mention that my mother wants to meet you?"

My steps faltered. "What? Your mother? Oh hell. She'll know that we're not *actually* engaged. Mothers have a sixth sense about these things."

He shook his head. "You don't have to lie to her. I told her the situation. Or at least most of it. But she won't get off my case until I present you."

"Xander, I dunno. I—"

"You'll meet her, and then she'll back off. Please?"

With one uttered word, I knew I couldn't deny him. "Why do I have the feeling that I'm going to regret this?"

Imani

The doorman greeted me with his usual cheery smile and Yorkshire accent. I still could barely make out the, "How are you, love?" But I smiled and answered with a distracted hello.

When the elevator dinged and opened at the penthouse level, I saw that Alistair waited for me outside our front door.

"A-Alistair, what are you doing here?"

He shook his head. "I didn't believe you actually lived here. When he commits to something, he really commits. I'll give him that much. Tell me, what's the plan? You stay 'engaged' for a couple of months, then you have a dust-up and it's Splitsville?"

Heat suffused my face. That was exactly the plan. "I don't know what you're talking about. I'm going to have to ask you to leave."

"I must say, you are certainly committed to the ruse. I'm sure Xander's reported prowess in the sack has something to do with it. He knows how to fuck women into a stupor. How does it feel to be one of many?"

Jutting my chin out, I glared at him. "Like I said, it's time for you to go." Quickly assessing the situation, I knew the elevator was my best bet to get away from him.

"I think I'll wait for Xander inside."

"I don't think that's going to happen, Alistair. You

and I both know how Xander feels about you. And frankly, you shouldn't be here. Isn't he at the office anyway?"

Alistair strode to me, standing directly in my path, blocking any access I had to the flat. I stood my ground and tipped my head up so our gazes would meet. I recognized the gesture. It was one of dominance, designed to make me cower.

Directors used it to convey who the aggressor was without actually stating it. "You need to back up about five feet, Alistair. I don't like being crowded."

His brows snapped down, and he looked confused for a moment but then backed up a couple of feet. Not far enough, as far as I was concerned, but it would do for now. Rolling my shoulders, I asked, "Do you have a message for Xander? Or would you like to wait *downstairs* for him to come home?"

"Do you even know the kind of man you agreed to marry? Do you know what he's capable of? The things he's done?"

He was going there? After what he'd done? "What about the things *you're* capable of? I know what you did to him. Your presence here is inappropriate. You need to go." He took a step toward me again and this time, I backed up toward the elevator.

"You think this is fucking inappropriate? Imagine

how I felt when he killed my father. And he's walking around free and clear for that. He robbed me of a *parent*."

My anger spiked. "Is that how you see it? What about what your father robbed him of. What *you* robbed him of?"

Again, Alistair staggered back.

"Yeah, that's right, he told me what you did to him. You could have helped him, but you didn't. You could have made all the difference, and you might still even have your father alive. But instead of aiding a helpless child, you held him down for your sick, psycho of a father. And then you tormented him as an adult. You're despicable. You went after his fiancée, and you deliberately ruined his world."

His face contorted with anger, and he lunged for me again. With a finger pointed in my face, each word he spoke was punctuated by spittle. "You don't know anything about my father. He was a great man. Shut your fucking whore mouth."

I squared my shoulders then wiped the spittle off my face. "First of all, say it, don't spray it. Secondly, I'm not a whore. I'm a woman who recognizes that you need help." Behind me, I frantically pressed the call button.

But this time he didn't back off. "I did Christie a favor when I warned her off. You're just too dumb to see what he is, who he is. Is it his skills in bed you're so enamored with? Or have those been greatly exaggerated?"

The next words tumbled out of my mouth before I could remember not to antagonize the crazy man. "Your wife should know, shouldn't she?"

His hands snapped around my neck so quickly I had no time to react. Immediately, the pressure blocked my airflow and I fought back, kicking my legs out as I clawed at his hands, but he was too strong.

"What the fuck did you say about my wife?"

Shit. You've done it now. "Nothing. I didn't say a thing."

He squeezed harder as he tried to pull me in tighter, his stale tobacco and gin breath making the bile churn in my gut. "That's what I get for marrying a whore. I knew, you know, how she was. When Xander told me, I knew it was true, but I didn't want to believe it. Well, he took my whore. Now I'm going to take his."

Everyone always thinks when panic sets in everything starts going at laser speed. But for me, my world slowed to a crawl, as if I could experience the space even between heartbeats. The space between each breath. I could feel it all as my brain sluggishly responded to the call for fight or flight.

Even the sweat popping out on my skin was slow to arrive, but when it did, it was first a flash of prickly heat then like someone had slapped a cold wet rag against my bare skin.

"You don't want to do this."

"You're right. I don't want to. But I will. If for no other reason than to tell him that I've been here. I'm sorry, but he won't want you afterward. I hope you've saved whatever he's been paying you, because he'll be done with you. You won't be worth anything to him. You'll be no better than those whores he frequents."

Fucking direct hit. His words hurt more than his grip did. There was no way in hell I was letting him know how close his words hit to home. Once I was no longer a novelty, would Xander be rid of me? Once he knew the secrets I kept, would he still want me?

Pain lanced through me. Time to get with the program. In the whole fight or flight response choice, I wanted flight. I desperately wanted flight. But I didn't have that option.

I had no way out. I'd mouthed off to someone who was, in essence, a psychopath, or at the very least extremely disturbed, and I hadn't planned my exit. *You know better. Always have your exits mapped out.*

But what was done was done. I could stand here, afraid, unable to move, or I could fight. I could refuse to let someone like him win. I might not make it out of this scenario alive, but I'd take a piece of his ass with me.

Let's err on the living through this side of the fight though, shall we?

When he still wouldn't release me, I swung out with my free arm. I knew my target, and it wasn't what most would think of. So, when he predictably moved backward out of the way of contact, the meaty open palm of my hand made contact with his ear.

His loud howl of pain as he released me to clutch his ear stunned me momentarily. I took a second too long to move. When I did, he grabbed me again, this time putting my throat in a chokehold.

"You know, I didn't see any pleasure in it before. But I've changed my mind. I'm going to enjoy hurting you."

I knew two things. The first being I had seconds to get out of this. The second being I could buy more time by turning my head into the crook of his elbow.

The only problem was that I couldn't remember enough of the rest of the defense move I was attempting, so all I managed to do was ineffectively tug at his arm. I mewled as the real fear set in.

"Shh, shhh, shh. Don't go all ineffectual on me now. I liked it better when you fought. Gives me something to work with. If you go all *close your eyes and think of England* on me, then I'm not only going to hurt you, I'm going to scar you."

He wanted to scare me. And it was working. I fought

harder, even as the wave of dizziness took hold. I breathlessly spat out, "Eat a bowl of dicks."

"There we go. Now that's the spirit."

The elevator dinged, and when the doors slid open, Alistair shoved me forward. I stumbled but didn't fall, instead hitting a wall of muscle. I was spun around quickly and settled into the furthest point of the elevator.

The next thing I knew, Xander had his fist jammed against Alistair's nose. His head snapped back, his hands flying to his face to stem the blood flow.

Xander's movements were so quick that Alistair barely had a chance to recover.

And Xander was not only quick, he was deadly. I slid to my butt and wrapped my arms around myself, squeezing into a tight little ball.

Completely ineffective and not any help at all. Forget kicking any kind of ass. Forget taking names. Hell, I was giving mine to anyone who wanted it. I was the exact opposite of badassery.

As I watched him, I understood just how deadly Xander could be after he delivered a knee to Alistair's midsection. Then, when the man doubled over, Xander hooked his thumbs into his eye sockets, forcing his head up and exposing his throat. Then he delivered a quick punch directly to the trachea.

Alistair collapsed in a heap at Xander's feet, clawing at his throat and wheezing.

Xander whirled on me. "Are you hurt?"

I dragged in gulps of air and shook my head. "I— I don't think so."

He approached me slowly, his hands out in front of him. "I'm sorry. This is my fault. I made him resign from the trust, and he flipped. I should have anticipated something like this."

I pushed to my feet before stumbling into his arms. His touch was gentle as he held me close. I let myself fall into his embrace and relaxed into his hold. But out of the corner of my vision I saw Alistair crawling toward the stairwell. "Xander. He's getting away."

He whirled around but didn't release me. "Let him go. You're the one I'm worried about right now. He'll get what's coming his way."

"I'm okay. I swear. Can we just go inside?"

"Right." He held my face gingerly "I'm so, so sorry. I never would have forgiven myself if anything had happened to you."

"I'm okay." If only that was true. Every time I blinked I could see Alistair with his arm around my throat.

Two hours later, after the police had come and gone, Xander settled me on the couch with tea and wrapped his arms around me. I automatically curled into his warmth. This was exactly where I belonged. He held me tight and whispered apologies as he kissed my temple. It wasn't long before I drifted off to sleep in his arms.

I wasn't sure what it was, perhaps Xander shifting to a more comfortable position on the couch, but something woke me. His voice was soft. "I know you were supposed to move out soon, but with Alistair out there, I want you to stay here until the police have him, okay? I won't forgive myself if something happens to you."

I tried to ignore the pang of disappointment. I wanted him to want me for the sake of wanting me. Not because he felt obligated. "Xander—"

"Please, Imani. I— I need you to stay here."

Was this his way of keeping me close? Did he want me the way I wanted him? "Okay."

I could feel the tension ebb out of his shoulders. "Good."

⚜

Imani

Hours after he'd taken me to bed, soft morning light filtered into his bedroom, rousing me out of a deep sleep. But sudden thrashing in the bed had me wide-awake.

"No. No, don't hurt me." The voice was so soft and

frightened I thought it was a movie. But I forced my heavy lids open. Xander lay next to me, tossing fitfully. He was having another nightmare. "Wake up, Xander. Wake up."

"I'm begging you. Please don't."

I couldn't reconcile the helpless voice with the man who clearly knew how to kill someone. I'd been terrified of the violence in him earlier. But instinctively, I knew he would never turn it on me. *Unlike Ryan.* He'd known how to not just incapacitate Alistair but how to kill him. If he had wanted to, he could have.

I wrapped my arms around the man I'd started to care about and shushed him, just like he had me, soothing him back to sleep. Was Alistair right? Was he a ticking time bomb? Was he a danger to me? *No. He wouldn't hurt you.* But he'd already proven he was capable of anything.

"Thanks for hanging out with me today."

I slanted Lex a glance. "I know this is a babysitting gig for you. You have no real desire to come to rehearsal. You know, you really don't have to do all this. I'll be fine. It's not like the police aren't on the lookout for Alistair."

Lex crossed his arms. "Let's just say that you're precious to Xander. And he'd rather keep you close until they find Alistair. So while he's gone, consider me your armed guard."

"You realize this is ridiculous, right?"

He shrugged. "He'd do it for me. Hell, he *has* done it for me."

I studied him for a minute. He was so like Xander in a lot of ways. Their eyes, their bone structure. It was easy to tell they were brothers. "Do you mind if I ask you something personal?"

He leaned back in his chair. "Okay."

"I know I'm way overstepping here, but I need to know how to help him better. I care about him, but I have no idea how to do that. He shuts down if I even so much as suggest he talk to someone."

"Let me guess— He says he's fine. The nightmares don't mean anything and he's dealing with it."

I nodded. "Yeah. That sounds about right." I blew a stray strand of hair out of my face.

Lex sat forward in his seat, his elbows on his knees. "He had it bad. So did I, but Xan, he had it worse. *Much* worse. He has cause to hate Alistair. Really good fucking cause. And I want to see that asshole burn as much as the next bloke, but my concern is primarily for Xander and what carrying around that hate is doing to him. I've been after him for years to talk to someone. Sometimes he relents and goes, but it doesn't last long. He insists he can take care of himself."

Shivering and rubbing my hands up and down my arms, I said, "I just want to help him."

Alexi's smile was slow, tipping up slightly at the corners. "You're doing it. He's already more open than he's ever been."

"I dunno about that. He keeps saying he feels like he's losing control around me."

"And for Xander, that could be a good thing. He spiraled out of control a few years ago. Took a while to get him back together again. But he's determined not to go back to that so he holds on tight to control, sometimes too tightly, trying to force things to go the way he wants when what he should be doing is talking through it."

"I don't understand how I can possibly be helping him."

"You make him feel what it's like to really care about something again. Love someone again. It makes him crazy. And it should. It's part of life. He thinks living is battening down the hatches, but it's not. He's got to let go to really live."

I stared at him in shock. "He doesn't love me."

Alexi cocked his head. "I wouldn't be so sure about that. You care about him, and he could use that. He's certainly not the easiest person in the world to love."

The real question was, could I help him?

11

XANDER

A ny good intentions I had flew out the window. Eventually, I'd stopped pretending I could resist Imani at all. It really was futile. Worse, everybody knew it. "You make me sound like a bloody sap."

"No, Romeo, I make you sound like a man in love." Abbie beamed. "I have to say, it looks good on you. I much prefer this version of Xan over the cocky, too-full-of-himself one."

"I'm not full of myself. I'm confident. I thought women liked that."

"We do. But it usually signals a bad boy who will care more about himself than he will about you. But that's not the case with Imani, is it?"

I rolled my eyes and signaled to Lord Darby's

assistant that we were ready for him. I knew I really didn't have anything to lose by saying it out loud. I'd be telling Imani as soon as we got back anyway. I wanted her to stay. Not just at my place but in my life more permanently. I wanted it all to be real. "And if I do care about her, what's the best way to go about telling her? I'm a bit out of practice."

"For starters you can be honest and just tell her. No games. Just honesty. She's a cool chick. She'll appreciate that."

Honesty. I could do that. Right? How hard could it be? "Thank you. I, uh… I appreciate it."

"Like I said, love looks good on you. The big, bad Xander Chase. Felled by a slip of a girl."

I laughed. "Isn't that the truth?" But all in all, I was pretty happy about it.

"Now let's get back to work, so you can earn your keep. I doubt the trust is going to pay to keep you in exotic sports cars. You need to sing for your supper."

"Got it." Then, because I really appreciated her help and I wanted her to know, I said, "I know I don't say it enough, or ever. And I've been a pain in your side since you arrived—"

"In my side? Try my a—"

I choked out a laugh. "Yeah, I get it. But anyway,

thank you. You've been a great friend. And you'll be an even greater sister."

She blinked rapidly. "If you make me cry and ruin Sophie's makeup job, she'll kill you."

"I believe it." I slung on my camera. "But honestly, though, I love you." The words tumbled out of my mouth before I could run through the ramifications of what I'd said. Shaking my head, I added, "Wait, it wasn't supposed to sound—"

Abbie held up a hand. "I know what you meant. And I love you too. You and I were never meant to be. It was always going to be Alexi."

"And he was the better man for it."

Her smile was soft and a little dreamy. "Yeah, he is. But to be honest with you, you never did love *me* in that way. You loved the *idea* of me. And that all started to go away as soon as Imani showed up."

"I guess when it's real you know."

"That you do." She squared her shoulders. "Now, can we go and turn a sow's ear into a silk purse with this daddy-daughter photo?"

"I'm not sure why they even hired me. I'll have to Photoshop the hell out of this thing to make either of them look good. They might as well have hired a painter."

Abbie hit me on the arm. "For once in your life, try to be nice, would you?"

"This is me being nice."

"Lucky for you, Imani makes you far more charming."

Yeah, lucky for me.

12

I would pay money to see the contented look on Imani's face forever. As I massaged one foot, both of her eyes rolled into the back of her head and a low moan escaped her lips.

My cock twitched to life. *Down boy, you've already had her twice tonight.* Since that first time, we hadn't been able to keep our hands off of each other. The moment I'd come home it had been my routine to go looking for her in the flat. And I almost always found her in the library.

That night, she was curled up on the window seat with her script in her lap, staring out at the Thames.

I'd meant to tell her I loved her. Meant to make dinner, do the whole romance thing. Of course, the moment she looked up and smiled at me, I forgot all about using my words, and instead dropped to my knees in front of her and hiked up her dress to taste her. I could still hear her moan my name as she came on my tongue. From there, our lovemaking was quick and frenzied and hungry. Sinking into her bare was like nothing else I'd ever felt in my life.

Afterward, I dragged her into the shower to clean up. And as a byproduct of her soapy tits and water sluicing over that perfect ass, I made love to her again. Slower this time, refusing to let go until she'd had two orgasms. It was like my body kept trying to make up for all the missed orgasms of my life.

"You know that look on your face is quickly becoming an addiction for me."

Imani burrowed under the throw, bringing more of her toned legs into my lap. "Yes, I think we've established that you like my O-face. Particularly as you keep telling me when we're making love."

I kneaded my thumbs over the ball of her foot, and she groaned again. "Too right. In case you haven't figured it out by now, I'll do anything to see that look on your face."

"Hmmm."

Her phone rang, and she reached for it.

"Just leave it, love. They can leave a message." I'd been gearing up to tell her how I felt. I'd lose my nerve if the mood around us dissipated.

"It could be Charles with something about rehearsal. Or maybe my sister." She winked at me. "Don't you stop, though."

Who was I kidding? I was a total chickenshit. "Yes, ma'am." It was so easy to be with her. Freeing. Light. Was this what I'd been afraid of all this time? Now that I had her, I certainly wasn't letting go.

But the moment she answered her phone, her face fell. Next thing I knew, she was pulling her feet out of my grasp. I felt the loss immediately.

"Dad, calm down. I can't understand what you're saying."

I ground my teeth together and sat up, frowning at her turned back. She spoke in a quiet tone, but I could hear everything.

"Calm down, Dad. *I* paid the mortgage. Ebony told me about the notices from the bank. How could you let it get that bad? No. Just listen to me... I can't... Tell me what for... I can't just... That was all I had."

When she began pacing, my gaze tracked her every movement from the natural sway of her hips to her gesticulations with her hands. Everything about her fascinated me. As for her father, the man was a leech, and he was using her feelings of guilt to turn the money spigot.

"Dad, I put money in Ebony's account myself, you don't need to worry about what she needs. I've taken—"

I'd given her ten thousand pounds for her to pose as my girlfriend. How was that not enough money? And how could a father not even ask his daughter what she was doing to get that money? How could *I* not even feel any guilt for what I'd asked of her?

Knowing I shouldn't be listening, I quickly checked the messages on my tablet. Clicking on the email message with the subject line *Status*, I sat back.

Garett Ball was very good at his job. Not to mention I was paying him enough to find Alistair. Not that I didn't trust the police could do their jobs, it was just that I didn't think their punishment would be swift or just enough.

"I found him. He's holed up in a grotty little bedsit in Hounslow. How do you want me to proceed?"

I tried to tune out Imani's conversation, but bits of it kept seeping in as she tried to determine just how much money her father needed. But her voice kept filtering in. I wanted to do more than just listen when she got a call like this. I wanted to fix it for her. But I knew how that would go. She'd refuse. As far as her family went, she wanted to take care of everything herself. Her damn pride wouldn't allow her to let me help her.

For once in my adult life, my wishes and actions didn't revolve around what I needed to do or my end goals. All I wanted to do was help her. And I knew how.

Maybe it was time to *show* her how I loved her instead of telling her. With a plan set in my mind, I typed out a quick response to Garett.

Can you leave word for those psychos in Pushka discreetly about his whereabouts and also tip off the police? We'll see who gets there first. Either way, he won't be our problem anymore. Then set up the jet and a flight plan. I'm taking a trip tomorrow. It'll be quick, so I'll need a pilot for the return too.

I hit send then tapped the home screen twice.

When Imani turned to face me, her features were drawn. Her normally smiling mouth was now flat and tight, and a line marred her smooth forehead. "All right?" I asked, even though I knew what the answer would be. She was nowhere near okay.

She sighed and let herself fall back onto the couch. "You don't have to keep asking."

"I think we've established I care about you, right?"

A ghost of a smile appeared over her lips. "Yeah, was that what we did that one time?"

"Cheeky." I brushed my hand over her hair. "I don't like seeing what it does to you every time you get a call from home."

She shook her head. "I'm sorry. I'm a total downer right now. I think I need to try to get home before the showcase. Dad lost his job and can't seem to keep it together for Ebony's sake. He fell behind on the mortgage and it took Ebony seeing the late notices from the bank for anything to be done about it. I'm afraid of how bad it's really going to get."

"I get the picture." One I didn't like. She'd been handling all of this on her own. Her sister was there, but Imani did her best to insulate everyone from what she felt were her problems to deal with. "But the showcase is in a week. I know, you say you don't want any help, but I have the means to help you. I wish you would let me."

She scrubbed a hand over her face, sending several strands of her thick hair swirling around her face. "Xander, we've been through this. As much as you want to control your environment, you can't control *this* situation. And they are *my* family to deal with. *My* problem, not yours."

It didn't matter how much I tried. She might say the words, give me her body, but there would always be a part of her that she kept to herself. And all I wanted to do was love her. *You could tell her that.*

"I'm not trying to take over. I'm trying to share the load. I know how heavy your rehearsals have been. This is the first night you've been home before me in weeks. You're stressed and you're even running your lines in your sleep. You've been doing press, and trying to make sure Ebony is good, and dealing with my special brand of crazy. Let *me* help *you*. For once, I'm not interested in doing the selfish thing, but you won't let me be selfless."

She sighed. "Xander, I'm thrilled you want to help, but the way I need you to be there for me is to hold my hand, and rub my feet, and feed me delicious food, and make love to me so I can escape for a few hours. That's what I need. I don't need a white knight."

I scooted closer to her and slung my arm around her shoulders. "I only want to help. I wish you would let me."

"I appreciate it." Imani leaned her head back and kissed my chin. "I really do. But I need to do this on my own. I just can't count on anyone else. I wish I knew how to lean on you, but I don't. It's not part of my makeup."

A fist tightened around my heart and squeezed. She might think she didn't need anyone's help, but she wouldn't be rid of me that easily.

⚜

XANDER

In the morning, I called Abbie from the plane. "Listen, I need you to handle my meetings today. I should be back in the morning, but if not, I'll need you to do the seminar class tomorrow as well."

There was a beat of silence on the line. "Sure. I can handle that. Is everything okay?"

"Yes, fine. I just need to sort out some things today."

"You want to tell me where you're going?"

The hell I did. "Not particularly."

She sighed. "Will you be off doing something you'll eventually regret?"

"Let's hope not."

She knew me too well. "This have anything to do with Imani?"

"What's with the inquiry? Look, all you need to know is I'll be out of town for the day. I'll be back tomorrow."

She sighed. "Don't do something stupid, Xander. You seem really happy with her. And I like her."

She did have a point there. Imani would be irate when she found out. But she'd have to see that I had her best interests at heart. And even if she didn't see it my way, at least I could take some of the pressure off of her. For weeks I'd watched her old man twist her up. If I could give her some peace of mind, then it was well worth it to have her mad at me for a while.

"I have no intention of mucking this up."

"Glad to hear it."

After disconnecting with Abbie, I settled in for a long flight with some work for the trust.

When I arrived at the airstrip in New York, a car was waiting for me. I gave instructions to the pilot for my return trip that night and made the two-hour drive to Imani's childhood home.

I was beyond knackered. And I still had work to do. I hadn't been lying when I told Lex that the trust did some good work. In particular, I cared about the work we did with at-risk youth and victims of sexual assault. It was the first time in a long time that the work I was doing mattered to the community as a whole, and it made a difference. I'd done charity work before, but never for something like this. Something that mattered to me.

I had thousands of photos to sift through from the benefit.

Collateral to approve, budgets to plan. I actually liked it. I'd always been the artist. It was nice to know my business brain worked just fine.

When I pulled up to the blue colonial, I noted the grass needed cutting, but for the most part the house was neat from the outside, and it wasn't hard to picture Imani growing up here. Maybe sitting on the porch swing in the summer with her friends or raking the leaves in the fall.

I needed to look her father in the eye when I told the old man to back off and give Imani some breathing room. After knocking, I waited for a couple of minutes, then knocked again. Finally, the front door opened and the man who stood in front of me was not what I'd expected. He had wild, lightly curling auburn hair, and his skin was cafe au lait. It was immediately clear where Imani got her hazel eyes from.

"Can I help you?"

"Hello. Are you Mr. Brooks?"

A frown creased the man's forehead. "What's this about? Who are you?"

"I'm Xander Chase. I'm a friend of Imani's."

Her father's brows arched, and he eyed me carefully, his gaze lingering on my watch, shoes, then finally over my shoulder at the Porsche Cayenne I'd rented. "Is that so? Then you know she's not here. She's away at school."

"I know, sir. It's you I'd like to talk to."

Her father crossed his arms over his chest. "Is that so? What is it exactly you want to talk to me about?" He didn't budge an inch, making it clear that he had no intention of inviting me inside.

Okay, so we were going to do this out on the porch? "The money she's been sending you and why it never seems to be enough. I'd prefer to come inside to discuss that, but if you want to do it out here, then we can."

That had the desired effect. With a sigh, her father stepped aside and let me in, taking me into the living room.

I glanced toward the kitchen and could see it was in

need of a thorough cleaning. In the living room, I sat on a floral-patterned chair that looked like no one had sat in it in years. "Sir, I won't take too much of your time. I understand you've got your hands full."

"Well, Imani left me to take care of her sister while she runs around doing God only knows what."

I locked my jaw. I would not get into a verbal sparring match with the man. I just needed to deliver a message. "Your daughter has been working really hard at school, and she's killing herself trying to take care of you here."

The older man scowled. "You say you're a friend of hers? With that accent and those clothes and that car, just what kind of friend are you? You don't look like a college boy."

Astute. "That's because I'm not. I'm just someone who's looking out for her."

"You've got that whole sugar-daddy vibe to you. Just what has my daughter gotten herself into over there? I knew it was a bad idea for her to go away to school."

I realized I might not make it through the afternoon without beating the man senseless. "I'm a man who cares about your daughter, and you need to listen to me."

"Just who do you think you are? You don't know anything about us or who we are."

"I know your daughter is breaking her back trying to

accommodate everything you need, from the mortgage to Ebony's extras to the car payments. I know she sent you money recently, but you've already called to tell her you need more."

"What do you know about it? She got a fancy scholarship and left us behind. Left me to cope with her sister. You don't know how hard it is."

"You're right. I don't. But I've had just a taste of how hard it is for Imani. So from now on, things are going to change."

"You have no right." Robert pressed a finger into my chest, and I could smell the gin on his breath.

"I have every right to protect the woman I love. And her family. Even if that means you. And since I don't have a lot of time, let me just tell you how it's going to be. First, I'm hiring a service to help around the house. They'll do the cleaning and stock the fridge with healthy food. Second, I have a friend who runs the Cedar Alcoholism Center not far from here. He's willing to take you on an outpatient basis. It comes with a sober companion who will live nearby."

Robert's face contorted from mild annoyance to a deep scowl as rage took over. "How dare you—"

"I can smell the gin on you. Let's save the indignation for when you're actually sober. And finally, your daughter Ebony. The Briarwood school in London has agreed to take her on as a student next year. And she'll be receiving a full scholarship, so there is no burden on you."

That last part had taken a hefty endowment and pulling of several strings. That and getting her school records were a bit tricky, but money was meant to be spent. And if Imani wouldn't spend it on herself, then I'd spend it on her family. Besides, I saw what it did to her to not have her sister close.

"I've also set up an account for you. Funds will be distributed to you weekly to cover mortgage and living expenses, including anything Ebony needs for school next year. If you exceed what's in there, you're shit out of luck. But if Imani calls, you're to tell her that you're just fine on cash. I don't give a fuck where you tell her it came from, but you will under no circumstances ask her for a dime ever again."

The older man's face grew red as he sputtered, "Who do you think you are?"

"I'm the man who loves her, and I'm not going to watch her kill herself trying to please you and fix a situation that's not her fault."

"So, you're just going to fix it for her?"

I curled then unfurled my fists, letting the anger course through me. I hoped I never got so defeated that I just gave up on everything, including my own daughter's happiness. "I would do anything just to see her smile. To remove any hurt or worry or pain from her eyes. I'd give my life to make that happen. So yes, since I have the means, I'm going to fix it. She's worth it."

Her father staggered back. "I—I never meant..."

"Save the apologies for your daughter. They're wasted on me."

"I love my daughter."

I chuckled. "If you say so."

"I do. You wouldn't understand."

I rounded on him. "I'll tell you what. If you love her, try being a father. Get yourself together. Sort yourself out. That's what she needs, not platitudes you don't mean. I'm giving you the means to pull up. Take it."

"And if I don't accept?"

"You don't really have a choice. The counseling is a requisite of you getting any money. Silence is also a requisite."

"She didn't know you were coming to do this?"

I met a gaze I knew well. "Do we have a deal, Mr. Brooks?"

We squared off for several minutes. Finally, Imani's father backed up. "We have a deal."

XANDER

"You're not slick, you know."

I took a sip of my wine as I studied Imani and my mother chatting away happily. Lex had taken a call, so that left Abbie free to interrogate me. "I'm not sure what you're talking about, Abena."

"And don't think you can do that thing that you do with your brother. You can't just use my given name and make me back off."

"Seriously, is this what having a sister is all about? Because I want a refund."

She smacked my shoulder. "Shut up. I can see how much you love her."

I gloomily stared into my wine glass. "Were you always this nosy? And I just didn't see it before?"

Abbie grinned. "Yep. You were too busy staring at my—"

I sputtered. "Jesus, Abbie!"

She blinked with mock innocence. "Pictures. What were you thinking?"

Despite myself, I laughed. "My poor brother. He's doomed for an early grave with you."

"Yeah, but he'll be laughing the whole way, won't he?"

"Probably."

She shifted from foot to foot before joining me on the window seat. "She has no clue what you did for her, does she?"

Now it was my turn to pretend ignorance. "What do you mean?"

"You're really going to lie to me?"

"I think you seriously overestimate my brain's capacity for intrigue. James Bond, I'm not."

"Tell that to Alistair. And shit, tell it to Easton. I don't think either of them will ever bother us again. Careful, Xander, or people are going to start thinking that you're the good guy. You might even be a hero."

"Bollocks. They'd be dead wrong. I'm a tosser. Completely."

"Yeah, sure you are. You're also the tosser who set up Imani's sister so she'd be close by. And I suspect you're also behind her father suddenly turning over a new leaf that she was telling me about."

I glanced down at my polished shoes. "I'm not that bloke, Abbie. You can try to make me out to be the good guy all you want. But that's just not who I am. Pub crawler, yes. Roguish photography professor, yes. I'm nothing more."

She shook her head. "I don't know why you like to pretend that you don't have a soft heart, but I know you. It's too late now. Once I've seen that side of you, it's hard to unsee."

I drained my glass and said the one thing likely to make her drop the subject. "So, you're saying if I'd done a nude photography class first you wouldn't be able to unsee that?"

Abbie sputtered and laughed. "Oh my God, you're impossible."

I took a small bow. "Where have I heard that before?" Imani laughed at something, dragging my attention back to her.

"My advice if you're open to it... Tell her you love her. Don't pretend with her. You deserve to be happy even if you don't think so."

Lex joined us and the lovebirds immediately intertwined their hands. "What are you two whispering about?"

"Oh nothing, just how much Xander loves Imani and how she's already changing him for the better."

Alexi raised his glass. "And they said it couldn't be done. Welcome to the dark side, brother."

I liked it on this side. I liked how I felt about her. But I had to mitigate the lies I'd told, or they were going to kill me. I didn't want to lie to her. But even more, I loved seeing her happy and carefree. I'd do anything to keep her like that.

13

I wiped my sweaty hands on my robe. *Relax, this is what you've been anticipating for months. You can do this.*

Three months ago, if anyone had told me I'd be the lead in this showcase and dating the hottest man I'd ever seen in my life, I'd have laughed. But this was it; I was so close to my dream. About to grasp it.

Now if only I had some family out there. I shook my head and continued my pre-performance pep talk. I wasn't going to worry about it. It didn't matter that my father wasn't there. Over the last week or so, he'd really been trying. He'd called to tell me he started an alcohol treatment program and he'd gotten another job. Facts Ebony verified.

It was like overnight a switch had been flipped. I

didn't trust it. He'd disappointed me enough in the past that I was wary. But I was willing to believe in the possibility of change. He wasn't thrilled that I was trying to move Ebony to London, but he was giving me less grief about it. So at least that was something.

I didn't have the money to bring Ebony just for the weekend, so my sister couldn't come either. Both Xander and Fe had offered to pay to fly her over, but I couldn't justify the cost just for my show.

I had friends, and they were my family now. And Xander, he would be out there. I smiled and slid a glance at the three dozen roses he'd had delivered. The first card had said break a leg. The second had pointed out all the places to shag in my dressing room. The final had detailed how he wanted to spread me out on the settee of my Fleet Street set and lick me until I begged for mercy.

That man knew how to make me blush and laugh and, most frequently, throw things. He'd been acting strangely for a few days, but when I asked him about it, he said it was work with the trust. I couldn't figure out what was bugging him. He told me nothing was wrong when I asked, but clearly, he wasn't his seemingly carefree self. It was more of a feeling than anything else. In bed, we'd been just as connected as we always were when he made love to me.

Even outside of the bedroom, things were good. We

dated. When he had time, he met me after rehearsal to walk me home. When he couldn't, he made sure there was a car for me. We had dinner with Abbie and Lex and our friends. I was pretty relaxed, even though I knew we would eventually have to deal with Alistair and figure our shit out.

We couldn't just play house forever. We both had some shit to work out. But I enjoyed every minute together, not taking a second for granted. I still hadn't told him how I felt about him, and I wouldn't be doing that anytime soon. He'd freak out and run.

But I would tell him. *Eventually*. But I knew something was bothering him, and I just wished he would talk to me. He hadn't had any more nightmares that I could tell, but he was off in some way. It was like he was trying too hard to keep something from me, though I hadn't had time to work through it all in my head. I'd get to the bottom of it after the performances. For the time being, I still had to focus.

There was a knock at my door, and I called out, "Come in."

Fe and all his fabulousness sashayed in wearing a dark blazer, cashmere slacks and the loudest, brightest paisley shirt he could probably find. "Darling, you look smashing."

I rolled my eyes and hugged him tight, careful not to

rest my cheek with all the stage makeup against his clothes. "Thank you for coming."

"Honestly. Where the fuck else was I going to be? You're my self-appointed little sistah."

I laughed. "But it's appreciated all the same."

"In that case, you'd better tear the roof off of this place, otherwise I'm disowning you."

"Oh, I will, and good luck with that. I hang on, spider monkey style."

"That's my girl. Go on, tell me— Any jitters?"

"Oh, you know, just the usual. Like there are hundreds of people out there who've come to see this, and I can't remember a single line, and holy fuck, I'll be naked on that stage."

Fe grinned. "I don't even like women, and I'm very excited about this proposition."

I smacked him. "Fe!"

He laughed and dodged another swat. "Relax, you'll be fine. You know this. You're ready. And remember, your fiancée is in the audience with another bouquet of flowers. I believe in you, and he believes in you. And you've got Abbie and the whole crew out there. We're here for you. You're not solitary Imani anymore. We are your family. You have this. I know this is a huge stretch for you, but you are incredible."

I loved him. I could always count on him to keep my mind calm. "Thank you, Fe."

"What are best friends for? Now, there's a very hot man out there dying to kiss you good luck. Can I send him back?"

My heart tripped into an immediate gallop. "Yeah, of course." The moment I saw him, I grinned. "I thought you were working late."

He raised a brow. "I lied. There was something I had to do. But there was no way I was going to miss this."

He wrapped his arms around me, and I finally relaxed. He was here. That was all that mattered. "What were you doing?"

"I'll tell you in a second, but first, a kiss."

One kiss from him and I'd relax… after he made me come half a dozen times. "Oh no you don't. I know all about your kisses. I'll be on the floor with my legs in the air before I know what's happened."

The Xander smile was in full effect. "C'mon, I'll be quick."

Laughing, I nuzzled him with my nose. "No dice. Besides, I'm all made up. I'll take a rain check for after, though."

He made a pouty face but tugged me close and kissed the end of my nose. "Since you won't let me have any fun, I have a surprise for you. Though I can't take full credit. This one is from both Fe and me."

"What is it?"

"Come on in," he called.

When the door opened, I held my breath, not sure what was happening. Ebony poked her head in. "Everybody decent? Fe warned me about the both of you."

Butterflies danced in my belly as my brain tried to reconcile what I was hearing with the truth I knew. "Ebony? What? How?"

My sister grinned. "You've been withholding, big sister. You should have mentioned your boyfriend had a private jet."

I turned on Xander. "You did this?"

He held his hands up. "Before you get all huffy, just know that Fe and I weren't going to let you go on stage without your sister and your dad."

I turned back to my sister. "Dad's here too?"

Ebony nodded. "Yeah, he's in the audience, but I couldn't wait to see you. Besides, I didn't want to take the chance you'd see us in the audience and forget your lines or something."

"That's a totally good call because I would have." I turned to Xander. "You shouldn't have."

"Woman, for once, just smile and say thank you. You can yell at Fe and me later. I just want you to be happy."

God, I loved him. "Thank you. You don't even know what this means. Ebs, how long are you staying?"

My sister slid Xander a glance. "Don't be mad at him. But I have an exam on Monday, so I have to go right back. We're leaving after the show."

"What? But that's not even fair. We have so much to talk about."

"I know, but at least I get to see you. And there's more good news."

I didn't think I could take any more. "What?"

"I got a call from Briarwood. I've gotten a special scholarship that will allow me to board. Full ride."

"Are you shitting me?"

"Nope. London is calling. Woot!"

I hugged my sister tight. "This is the best news in the world. We're going to have so much fun."

"I know it."

There was another knock at my door. "Call time, five minutes."

I didn't want them to go, but I had work to do. "Be right there."

I hugged my sister again and Ebony left me and Xander alone. He kissed me soundly, his lips crushing mine. His tongue slipped into my waiting mouth with sure strokes, and I immediately forgot to be nervous. All I felt was electricity, and energy, and humming need. He pulled back, panting, and his lips were covered in my red lipstick.

"I'll get out of your hair. I just wanted to tell you one thing."

He had something else to tell me besides how much he wanted me? "Oh yeah, what's that?"

"I'm proud of you."

"Thank you, Xander."

"You have no reason to be nervous because you're going to kill it. I fell in love with you the moment you slipped into character, and the rest of the audience will too." He then kissed me on the forehead and walked out.

My knees wobbled, and I braced a hand on my chair to steady myself. That idiot had love-bombed me and run.

14

IMANI

S o this was what freedom and happiness felt like. Excitement coursed through my veins as giddy happiness skipped along my synapses. There was nothing like the high from a performance. The audience had given me a standing ovation. *Me.* Holy hell. Charles had been yammering about how I needed to gear myself up because I'd be too busy to even think over the next few months.

With the music Jasper was spinning blasting out of every speaker and my new friends all dancing and laughing, I felt alive. At the bar, Xander spoke to Alexi, laughing at something his brother said. Suddenly he looked up and caught my eye. The grin he gave me was wide and unguarded. I finished my drink and leaned over to Fe. "Listen, I'm going to try to drag my boyfriend out of here for some wild sex. You okay here?"

Fe whooped. "It's about fucking time. Go shag your brains out, miss theater star."

I laughed and took a gulp of Fe's drink. Since the crowd consisted of the cast and crew and our friends, people made room for me easily. When I reached the two Chase brothers, my stomach gave a hint of a flutter. "Excuse me, Alexi, but if you don't mind, I'd like to drag my boyfriend off for a shag."

Xander sputtered, spraying his drink. Alexi's laugh cracked through the air like a whip. "Finally, a woman who knows how to take my brother well in hand. You two kids have fun."

I reached for Xander's hand and threaded my fingers though his. "You ready to get out of here?"

His lips turned up at the corners in that slight smile that drove me nuts with desire. "You realize you'd be running from your own party, right?"

I nodded. "There's something else I'd rather be doing right now."

"I'm not daft enough to argue with a beautiful woman. Let's go home."

That's where my plan tilted on its rails a little. I had no intention of going home. I wanted to be adventurous with him. Wanted to be spontaneous. "Who said anything about wanting to go home?"

Xander cocked his head as if needing clarification. But his eyes had darkened to almost black. He knew exactly what I wanted. "Imani." The way he said my name sent a shiver through me. It held promise of seduction and fun and satisfaction. But he still seemed hesitant when he leaned in to whisper close to my ear. "All your friends are here. And this is a very public place."

"I don't care. For once I want to throw a little caution to the wind."

His gaze dipped to my lips, and I could feel the rumble of his chest against mine.

"I don't want the possibility of anyone interrupting us. I want you all to myself."

How could I possibly convey what I wanted? The alcohol was fuzzing my brain just a little, and I inhaled deeply to try to clear it so I could make him understand. "I want you. I want you to see me as sexy and spontaneous and adventurous. You've had—" I cut myself off and tried for better words. "I want to try something different. Give you something. You've implanted me into this fairy tale for weeks now, and I just want to show you how that makes me feel." Fuck, I was getting this wrong. "You've had a lot of women, and I know you—"

He pressed his thumb to my lips when he lifted his hand to caress my face. "Would you stop? One woman or a hundred—not a single one has come close to making me feel what I feel with you. I don't need you to try to be anything else. All I want is you. However you'll have me."

I tilted my chin up. "And if I said I wanted you now? And it turned me on to sneak off with you? I want you so hot for me that you can't be in control."

&

Xander

I was a coward, and I knew it. After I'd dropped my love bomb, I'd retreated quickly to the safety of the front row to avoid her response. If she didn't love me back, I didn't want to know, at least not right away. I wanted to pretend for the rest of the night. And if she did love me, well, then I'd feel even guiltier for not telling her I'd gone to see her father.

But it was hard to think about anything as Imani danced in front of me. My semi-erect cock went instantly rock hard when she ground her ass into me. Fuck. Just thinking about my fingers slipping through her wet sex made me throb.

The throng of people dancing around us and the knowledge in her eyes of what she was doing to me made me even hotter. We were in plain sight, but I loved feeling like that with her. Knowing that I could make her so needy she forgot who she was, where she was.

She leaned back into my chest as her ass ground onto my cock. "You dropped a bomb then ran from me. I thought we had an arrangement to stay and deal with things."

Oh yeah. Just the first of many promises I'd broken. I swallowed hard as my brain scrambled for what I could possibly say. "I know." She canted her hips, popping her ass right into my cock again, and my eyes crossed. Of course it prompted an image of me taking her while standing. Maybe she'd even let me have her ass. Just the thought had the base of my spine tingling. "Imani, fuck." She was doing what she accused me of doing. Using sex to control me.

She turned in my arms and cupped my cheek. "Xander." Her voice was soft. "Please, look at me."

"What?"

"I love you too."

I stilled. "What?"

"You heard me. I love you. And if you'd given me half a chance earlier, I would have told you so. And total dick move telling me right before I had to go on stage, by the way."

She loved me? Slowly, understanding of what she'd

said seeped into my consciousness. She *loved* me. I wasted no time dragging her through the club to the stairs. When I reached the top, I went first. When I was sure we were completely alone, I locked the door. There were perks to being VIP.

Dragging her to the central bench overlooking Mayfair, I kissed her hungrily, stroking deep into her mouth, sliding my tongue against hers. My hands were desperate to be on her, and I gripped too tight. Her gasp of shock had me gentling my hands and my kiss.

I slid my lips over hers in a barely-there caress, relishing how soft she was. Her tongue dipped out to tease. Muffling a moan, I kissed her a little deeper, chasing her tongue. Grinding my hips against hers. My cock was like a rocket primed and ready to go.

With a series of tears and contortions, she got my shirt off then helped me with the buckle of my belt, then my jeans, managing only to get them shoved over my ass and freeing my aching erection.

I knew what she was going to do. And I backed up onto the bench to brace myself. There was no way I was going to survive her mouth on me. The anticipation was enough to kill me.

When she lowered herself between my strong legs, I gripped my cock at the base, ready to feed it to her. "You're sure you want to do this, Imani?"

Slowly, she nodded. "I've been wanting to try this for a while now. But you're always too impatient."

"That's because your pussy is like a velvet vise. Hand to God, it's my favorite place to be."

"You know, I don't think I said thank you properly for bringing my sister and father to my show."

I bit my bottom lip. "By all means, thank me."

Imani wrapped her lips around my cock, and I wanted to go off before her tongue even started to lick me. She hollowed her mouth out as she sucked me deep, cupping my balls at the same time.

"Oh shit. Imani… Fuck. Jesus. Fuck me."

She alternated stroking me with one hand while she licked the length of me, paying particular attention to the underside, with deep pulls into her mouth. But it was when she massaged my balls and scraped my perineum with her fingertip that my control snapped.

I gripped two handfuls of hair and lifted my hips to control her movements. But it didn't matter how crazy she made me; I was careful with her. Not pushing too far. When she released my balls and used both hands to stroke me in time with her mouth, my vision crossed. "Imani, God. You have to stop, I'm going to—"

She sucked harder, coating my cock with saliva. But it wasn't until she gently scraped her teeth just over the tip that I erupted, all brain functions ceasing.

15

It had taken more than fifteen minutes for me to be able to walk again, let alone talk or provide anything useful to a conversation. There on the roof, under the stars, I held Imani tight, unwilling to let her go. She loved me. And deep down I knew it was true. I also knew that I'd never properly loved anyone outside of Lex before. I could be a selfish bugger, and most things were all about me. With Imani, that was different.

When she stirred, I kissed her temple. "You realize you've completely broken me, right? I can't talk, hell, I can barely move."

She lifted her head and grinned up at me. "So, you like how I said thank you?"

Hell yes, I liked it; I fucking loved it. But something about what she said gnawed at me. "You know, you didn't have to blow me to say thank you. I just wanted to make you happy."

"Xander, I know. I'm teasing. I wanted to try something new in a, uh, new environment. And I wanted to blow your... mind."

The laugh bubbled out of me before I could contain it. "My mind, huh? Consider it blown. But since this is your party, how about I take you back downstairs so you can enjoy it."

"I'd rather stay with you."

I groaned. "You say things like that and I'm liable to go back to my selfish ways and keep you all to myself."

She shrugged before snuggling back into me. "What's wrong with that?"

"Oh no you don't. Plenty of time for that when we get home. And for the record, you'd better get your fill of your friends tonight, because I plan on keeping you in bed for a very long time. They might not even recognize you when I finally let you out, it'll be so long."

"Promises, promises," she laughed. "You'll be the first one to complain about needing sustenance."

"This is London. Everywhere delivers."

She rolled her eyes, but she eventually stood and tugged me to my feet. The smile she gave me was so unguarded that I fell in love all over again. "You were fantastic tonight. Just in case I didn't say that already."

Imani ducked her head. "You did. Thank you."

"Well, it's the truth. When you get up on stage, I cannot take my eyes off of you."

"And how is that different from any other time?"

I laughed, for the first time in a long time feeling truly light. "It's not. But it's especially true when you're on stage. You're beautiful to watch." With little effort, I wanted her again. I wanted to spread her out on one of these benches and show her all the ways I could love her. But I recognized what that feeling really was; I wanted to feel close to her, to see her happy. But I knew enough now that I could also do that without sex. My cock, of course, complained. *Wanker.* "Come on, let's go."

When we returned downstairs, the party was in full swing. Nick and Fe had sandwiched some girl and were grinding to some dance track Jasper was playing. Several of the cast members had started dancing on the low tables around the VIP section. Some had already started dancing on the platforms on the back of the seating area. Since it was a private party, no one would complain. And well, I'd paid enough to rent the VIP room for that purpose.

Imani was immediately surrounded by Abbie, Faith, and Sophie and dragged off to the dance floor. I'd even invited Miriam, who sat at the bar with a friend holding court. I owed her more than she knew. Without her, I wouldn't have Imani.

"I saw you and my girl vanish earlier." Ryan knocked back the amber liquid in his glass.

I gritted my teeth. If I'd had my way, Ryan wouldn't have been invited. But he was part of the cast. I was just happy that after their show tomorrow Imani wouldn't have to see him again. "Saying she's your girl implies that she can actually stand you. And both of us know that's not true."

"She likes me enough to not quit the show. What you and she don't understand is that she never got over me. Why else would she stay if she hated me so much?"

"You're pissed." And I wasn't pissed enough to keep talking to this git and not care.

"How does it feel to know you have my scraps? The great Xander Chase with my sloppy seconds. Though, I don't know how you can stand the cold-fish routine with her just lying there. Fuck, and then the crying afterward." Ryan's words slurred together, and my hands twitched with the urge to hit him.

"Shut the fuck up."

Ryan put up his hands, then weaved, then listed to the left a little. "Don't be mad at me, mate. Just telling you like it is. And a piece of friendly advice; I'd get your slander lawyer ready, because the moment things go bad, she'll start screaming rape. You won't even get a chance to explain."

I froze. "What the fuck did you say?"

Ryan stumbled backward again, and his words jumbled together. "She's lying. I didn't hurt her. I *loved* her, you know? She'd been teasing me for a year. And she wanted it to happen. Then after, she said I forced her. Fuck that slag."

Fury set my blood to boiling, but it also temporarily immobilized me. "I will fucking kill you."

But Ryan seemed unconcerned. "You have to ask yourself why she kept coming to rehearsals with me. She saw me every day. It was because she still has feelings for me. I didn't do what she said. Then you swooped in and started interfering with my plan to get her back." He stumbled forward with a wild swing.

Finally, I snapped out of the frozen fury. My knuckles connected with Ryan's jaw in the blink of an eye. Recoiling quickly, I hit him again. And again. And again, letting out the anger and the fear and the panic. This asshole had hurt Imani, and now I was going to hurt *him*. And soon, I wasn't seeing Ryan any longer. I was seeing Silas and Alistair. Ryan feebly tried to land a punch or two, but I didn't stop until someone strong grabbed me from behind.

"Xan, fucking stop it." Lex's voice in my ear.

I struggled, but Lex didn't loosen his hold on me. "Sod off. Let me go."

Lex dragged me forcibly into a back room to the right of the stairs. "I'm not letting you go until you bloody calm down. What the fuck is the matter with you?"

Still seething, I shouted at my brother. "He hurt her, Lex. He fucking hurt her."

"Who?"

"Imani. That asshole hurt her."

Lex's voice went flat. "What do you mean he hurt her?"

"He as much as admitted to raping her. The fucker is so twisted he thinks he cares about her."

Lex released me. "Son of a bitch."

"Now you see why I was kicking his arse."

Lex scrubbed a hand over his face. "Yes, but you can't do this here. Not in front of all these people. I saw him take a swing at you. That's why I came over. But you obviously didn't need my help."

I leaned against the wall. "For fucking once, right?"

"Xander." Lex shook his head. "As much as you want to kill him, you can't. He's not Silas or even Alistair."

"Would you be so fucking calm if this was Abbie? If you'd been the one to find Easton?"

Lex shook his head. "No. But then I'd count on you

to keep me from killing the bloke. You need to get out of here and cool off. I'll take care of Ryan."

"Lex..." I wasn't going to let my brother save the day.

"Alexander," Lex said more firmly. "Get some air. It's not the end of the world. Let me help."

Everything inside me shriveled. That twat had hurt her. And she'd never told me. Worse, day after day, she'd gone to rehearsal, putting herself in harm's way. *She never told you. That's not love.* I needed to get out of there. "You're right. I need air."

"What do you want me to tell Imani?"

I shook my head. "Don't tell her anything."

IMANI

I let myself back into the flat. I'd spent the whole morning out looking for Xander. How could he just abandon me last night? Lex had told me that Xander left but hadn't said why or where he was going. Not long after, I saw Ryan being carted out with a black eye and a bloody nose.

I'd tried to call and text, but my texts went unanswered and my calls went straight to voicemail. Was this how it ended? He'd just vanish on me? I'd gone over the possible scenarios a million times over. Had he just been waiting for me to say the words? Was it all a game to him? But that made no sense. He'd said he loved me and looked terrified when he'd done it. He'd looked even more scared when I had said it back.

Maybe he hadn't thought I would. Maybe he hadn't meant to say it at all. He thought he could say it and pretend it had never happened? None of it made any sense at all. I needed to talk to him. Lex, unfortunately, was no help. I'd gone to the barge first thing that morning to see if he'd turned up there, but I'd only found Abbie and Lex. No sign of Xander. And while I thought Lex would cover for him, I was pretty certain that Abbie wouldn't. Hell, she'd wanted to come hunt him down with me.

My next stop had been to check the Notting Hill flat, but no one answered. Granted he could have been on the other side with another girl. My stomach twisted at the thought. No. I was going to choose to believe that he loved me. *Then where the hell is he?*

I'd even gone to my place and checked to see if he was there, just in case he'd assumed I went home and was looking for me. But he was nowhere to be found.

After tossing my keys on the kitchen counter, I dropped my purse on the couch and toed off my shoes. I'd been so worried the night before that I sat up all night waiting. I'd only washed my face and tossed on some sweats. Maybe after a long, hot shower I'd figure out where to look next.

As I stepped into the hallway, I heard the shower going in Xander's bedroom. Heart stuttering into a gallop, I ran down the long corridor, calling for him. "Xander? Are you in there?"

The bathroom door was ajar, and I could see him in the shower. One arm braced against the wall, the other— What the hell— Was he? Oh yeah. His eyes were screwed shut, and he ran a soapy hand over his massive, pulsing erection.

I stood on the threshold watching him, his strong body doing one of the things he did best. The man was made to have sex. But the tight lines around his mouth told me he wasn't enjoying himself. The rapid, jerky movements looked more like punishment.

I shed my clothes quickly and opened the door to the giant shower stall. Xander's eyes flew open, and he staggered backward. "Imani, what the fuck are you doing?"

"I'm giving you a hand. You look like you could use one."

His hands shook, even as his cock bobbed in front of me. "You should go."

"And what? Run away like you did last night? You can't run me off. You think I don't recognize that you're pulling away? I'm a master at it. But I love you, and I'm not going."

Xander shook his head and backed up another step. "No. Don't touch me. I'm not in a good place. I don't want you to see me like this."

I very deliberately stepped into his space. "Like what, Xander?"

He backed up again but hit the wall. "Fucking broken, Imani. If you touch me, I don't know what will happen."

"I have a pretty good idea. We'll make love. And then we'll talk about why you ran out on me and left me there alone. And we'll also talk about why you let me worry about you half the night and day. But as you like to say, we're going to fuck first and talk later, because despite all that, I still want you. I still need you."

"Imani." My name sounded like a plea on his lips.

But I was in no mood to let him run from me again. I'd opened myself up. It was too late for me; I loved him. I wasn't going to let him run. "Touch me, Xander."

⚜

XANDER

I shook. Even with makeup smudges under eyes and her hair a wild tangle of curls, I wanted her desperately.

I'd spent the night at a hotel trying to get my mind around what the hell had happened to her. The things I'd done and said to her.

I felt like shit about it all. And worst of all, there was still a need to do some serious violence coursing through me. I needed to let the tension out before I could talk to her, help her.

But I was also furious with her. How could she not tell me? How could she keep putting herself in harm's way? It was like she had a death wish. Or didn't care that I'd be shredded if something happened to her.

Now she was standing in front of me asking me to fuck her first. *Shit.* We were so fucked up. But I needed her too. There was no way I was turning her down. I prayed I had the control she needed from me.

"Turn around."

She complied with no resistance, bracing herself against the wall, the shower spray soaking her hair. Water sluiced down her arched back, and her ass canted upward as if on offer from the gods.

With one swift step forward, my cock twitched against her, and I adjusted my hips so that I nudged her pussy.

My name came out on a whisper, and she pushed back against me. I didn't need the lube I'd brought into the shower with me. She was wet, slick for me as if she'd been waiting for me to come home just for this.

She moved her hips back, and my dick slid into her moist depths easily. *Home.* Fuck. How could she love me? She had no idea what I'd done. I wanted to hold on to her forever now that I'd found her, but why would she want that? How could she want to be with me?

Reaching around her body, my hand sliding down her taught belly, I slid my fingers into her slick folds, seeking her clit. When I found it, I pressed gently and rubbed circles with a slow, well-practiced precision. "Oh, Xander. OhmyGod. OhmyGod. OhmyGod."

Her inner walls milked me tight, and the blissful spread of my orgasm started in my toes as always, and I leaned into the release, desperate for it. Desperate to bond with her, but the more I chased the orgasm, the more elusive it became.

Gritting my teeth, I sank into her hard enough for her to gasp, and my fingers dug into her flesh, pinning her in place, ripping another orgasm from her. Never yielding my motions over her clit.

"Please, Xander, I can't take any more."

"Yes, you can," I growled. "Give me another one." But even as I insisted on pulling another orgasm from her, I felt nothing. I knew there was no release waiting for me on the other side. The orgasm I'd been chasing had dissipated into thin air.

Closing my eyes tight, I pictured her smiling face as she danced around the living room. And the way she chewed on her bottom lip when she was working out a problem. Or the way she voraciously attacked food. The problem was that thinking about all the reasons I loved her only made me harder. Throb more. Made my skin, tighter. *Fuck*. I forced myself to pull out, even as my cock protested.

"Xander," she begged.

I dropped my forehead to her shoulder and kissed her. "Yes, angel?" The endearment slid off my tongue with ease. I reached over and grabbed the lube I'd brought in with me. I wanted all of her. Needed all of her. I had to find some way to erase the memory of what Ryan had told me.

Gently, I pressed a lube-slicked finger between the seam of her ass, rubbing it over the tight pucker, pressing slightly. She gasped at first, then moaned my name as my finger slid past the tight ring of muscle.

I was barely able to tear the words out of my throat. But I would rather die than hurt her. "This okay?"

Imani nodded even as her eyes fluttered closed. Neither of us spoke. Only the sound of the water hitting the tiles and our panting filled the silence. I readied her gently, taking my time, adding one finger, then another, stretching her. I was careful with her, even though I was way past the point of desperation.

Lining my cock up to her now-slick asshole, I pressed. She tensed immediately, and I stilled. The last thing I wanted to do was hurt her. When she turned to face me again, she bit her lip. The look of need mixed with a hint of fear softened some of the hard edges driving me on, and I kissed her lips.

When she relaxed, her body softened, and the head of my cock slid in easily. Fuuuck, that was good. *Too good.* Reaching around her, I held on to her breast with one hand and stimulated her clit with the other. The tight grip of her ass on my dick hurtled me toward that release that I chased. But the deeper I sank into her, the harder the demons rode my back, taunting me.

She'll leave you when you tell her. She's not yours. She doesn't know the kind of man you are. About the blood on your hands. You think she'll stay with you after she finds out?

I gritted my teeth and held her close. In the distant echo of my mind, I heard her chanting my name over and over and over again as I slowly fucked her ass. My body surged into hers, taking her, claiming her.

Her orgasm slammed through her, and I grunted when her body fisted around me like a vise grip. Spasming around me over and over again as she rode the wave, Imani went limp in my hands. But my hard-on still raged, throbbing and aching and wanting more. With long, measured strokes I fucked her ass, barely keeping hold of the slippery grip I had on my control.

Her voice was soft when she called my name on a moan. "Xander. I love you. I love you." She repeated it over and over and over again, bonding me to her with her words until the control slipped right out of my hands.

With a grunt, I fisted one hand in her hair and inter-twined the fingers of my other hand with hers on the wall.

She lowered our joined hands to her clit, and we stroked together. I followed her lead happily and reveled in the slickness coating both our fingers. She came again, her body sagging against the wall. And finally, I followed suit, my cock pulsing and expanding with each shot of my release deep inside her.

<hr/>

XANDER

I didn't know how long we stayed that way. Certainly, long enough for the water to cool. When I pulled my softened dick from her flesh, she hissed. I wanted to ask if she was okay. Wanted to know if I'd hurt her. Mostly I wanted to hold her. But the clawing need had receded.

Now we'd have to talk—the part I wasn't very good at.

We both cleaned off silently then wrapped ourselves in fluffy white towels before padding into the bedroom.

Once we were dressed, she sat on the bed and looked up at me, so I followed her lead. I was careful not to sit too close, lest I touch her again and forget that we couldn't solve everything with sex. I wanted more from her.

"Where did you go last night?" she asked.

So, we were jumping right in. "I stayed at a hotel after I took care of some things."

"I was worried. I looked everywhere. I even went to the Notting Hill flat."

I flinched. Did she really think I'd take someone there?

Of course, fucker. Why else would she go there?

"I wasn't there."

She shrugged. "Well, I didn't really have a lot to go on." I scrubbed a hand over my face as she continued. "You have to talk to me, Xander. Otherwise this won't work. Please." She reached out and took my hand, squeezing tight.

I shook my head. "Lex was fucking right. About all of it. He said the hate would eat me up from the inside, and now I'm not seeing straight."

"What you feel is understandable, Xander, but you can't let it control your life. Look, Alistair is gone. He's in the wind. You said so yourself. He won't bother us anymore. He knows I know about your past, and I didn't run. He has no reason to come back."

The lies I'd told were coming back to haunt me. "No, Imani. He's not just gone. It's probably more permanent than you think."

"What?" she whispered.

The disbelief on her face would turn to hatred, but I knew I had to tell her. "Still think you love me? I knew Alistair had embezzled money from the trust accounts. He owed money to fucking Pushka, the Russian mob. Since Trident Media is in trouble, he couldn't pull money out of there without looking suspicious. I cut off his means to make money by announcing the sale and breakup of his company. And then I told Jean what he'd been up to at the trust. I systematically dismantled his life."

"Xander, that's understandable after what he did to you."

"Do you know Pushka are well known for their torture tactics? I subjected another man to that. A human being. But I didn't care. What the fuck is wrong with me?" I could taste the salt of my tears. And the problem was that once I started talking to her, I couldn't stop.

"There's blood on my hands, Imani. You can't love me. Not after what I've done."

She squeezed my hand. "Alistair was a violent asshole who threatened my life. I don't know what he would have done if you hadn't come home that night. So I'm good with whatever you did to him. He made his own bed. You need to cut yourself some slack."

I pulled my hand away from hers. "How can you cut me any slack after what I just did to you?"

"What are you talking about?"

"Jesus, Imani." I pushed to my feet and started pacing. "I wasn't exactly gentle in the shower just now. And the shit I made you do… after what I now know."

She shook her head. "You didn't hurt me. I needed to be with you as much as you needed me."

My body vibrated. "Ryan told me last night. I know what he did to you. And even though I knew, I—I still did that to you."

She curled her body into herself and hugged her knees to her chest. "Oh God. He told you?"

I felt like my heart was tearing out of my chest. "Yeah. Why didn't you say anything to me?"

She swallowed hard, but her voice was very calm. "Xander, it was my problem to deal with."

A sudden flash of anger had me lashing out at her. "You went to rehearsal with him, every *fucking* day. Do you understand the dangerous risk you took? Maybe you were safe during rehearsal, but what about after? What about on breaks when he could have found any number of reasons to get you alone? Do you even care that I love you? What was I supposed to do if anything happened to you?"

"I had it under control. I spoke to Charles, and we were never alone together. I was as safe as I could be."

"Why would you even agree to work with him, Imani?"

"You say it like I had a choice. He has an established career. And he got cast after I did, which meant Charles wanted a draw. I wasn't enough. This is my livelihood. I tried to talk to Charles, but Ryan had already beat me to it. He wouldn't have believed me."

All I felt was pain radiating through my body, for her, for myself, for the things we'd been afraid to say to each other. "*I* would have believed you. *I* would have done something about it. Fuck, I did do something about it. Why wouldn't you tell me? After everything I've told you. After everything we've already been through together. Why?"

Tears tracked down her cheeks. "You don't understand."

I planted my feet on the hardwood floor. "You're shitting me, right? *I* of all people *would* understand. You say you love me, but that doesn't extend to letting me get too close. God forbid you ever depend on me for *anything*."

She stood as well, but instead of pacing, she wrapped her arms around her body. "That's what this is really about? Xander, I can't let you fix my life for me. After Ryan, I had to learn to function again. I needed to learn to get out of bed every day. To *not* be a victim. If I had quit the show or refused to work with him, he would have won. And what were you going to do, anyway?"

What I'd already done. I'd gotten infinitely more satisfaction from beating the shit out of Ryan than I had making Alistair pay. "I would have encouraged you to go to the police. I would have encouraged you to talk to someone." I ran my hands through my hair. "Fuck, I wouldn't have been such a fucking maniac with you. Jesus Christ, I've been so rough with you. I've made you *do* things." My stomach rolled as I thought of what we'd done at the club and just now in the shower. "Fuck, *just now*."

Imani placed her hands on my shoulders and shoved me. "Stop it. I wanted everything that happened this morning. From the second I met you, I knew you wouldn't hurt me. And you've proven time and again that if I say no you'll respect that. I couldn't be with you if that weren't true." She swiped at the tears on her face. "I've never felt like that in my whole life. Desired and free and in control of my sexual destiny. I *need* to feel that. I need to be desired and to feel like I'm in control."

"Imani…"

She shook her head, and her lips took on a determined slant. "You're not going to take that away from me. Maybe subconsciously it's one of the reasons I didn't tell you about Ryan. I don't want to be treated with kid gloves. I don't trust many people in my life, but I trusted you. Enough to fall in love with you."

"All I want to do is help you. I'm not trying to take away your control. Why can't you see that?" She was the most infuriating woman I'd ever met. How could she not see how much I loved her?

"The same goes here. I've watched you struggle with your nightmares for weeks. You refuse my help. You refuse to go talk to someone. Does that mean you don't love me like you say?"

"That is bullshit, Imani. This is different. Shit, your damn pride gets in the way of everything. If you took a second, you'd let people do things for you. Fuck, I've been trying to find a way to tell you for a week that I went to see your father without you flipping out on me."

Eyes wide, she met my gaze again. "You did what?"

I set my jaw. "I did what needed to be done." I was shouting, but I didn't care. "I was trying to do right by you when I went to see your father. And with Briarwood.

It's all I want, to take care of you, to love you. Why won't you let me?"

A frown creased her brow, and she shook her head. Short little jerky motions sent her soaked curls flopping into her face. "You went to see my father? Why would you do that?"

I gritted my teeth. What I wanted to do was say I was sorry for betraying her trust. Instead, I said, "You were being irrational. I have the means, so I took care of it for you. Now all you have to do is enjoy your sister and not worry about a loan."

"Those were *my* decisions to make. I took pride in being able to do it on my own, and you took that away from me.

My head throbbed. How had this gotten so fucked up? Why couldn't she see that what I'd done was for her? I was losing her. I knew if I kept pressing this she'd be gone. I needed to figure out a way to get her to stay. Problem was I could see it. I was making her unhappy.

"What do you want from me? Just tell me and it's yours. I'll give it to you to make you happy."

She lifted her chin and met my gaze. "Be open and honest with me. No more secrets. Share yourself with me and don't try to control me. No manipulation. Just love me."

My mouth dropped open. I knew what she wanted.

Me to be someone else. I'd bared my soul, and she'd been hurt.

I couldn't give her what she needed, and we both knew it.

We were going to break each other if we kept on like this. I knew I was ripping my own heart out with my bare hands, but it had to be done. "Maybe we need a break." Her head snapped back as if I'd slapped her, and I could feel every piece of my heart shatter.

When she spoke, her voice was tinged with steel.

"Fine. Maybe we do. Because it's clear that neither one of us knows what love is."

16

After my fight with Xander, I went home. It was where I belonged anyway. I'd only been playing house with him, but it was nice to pretend. It should have been a relief to sleep in my old bed with the aroma of vanilla filling the apartment. My first stop had been Fe's, but he wasn't home. Likely he was at Adam's.

I'd slept fitfully and woken up just after eight. My schedule was mostly clear until five when I had to report to the theater for our second show. All morning I waited for an angry call from Charles or Ryan, but nothing. And frankly I was too chickenshit to call them. I'd have to sweat it out until it was show time. No matter what I tried to concentrate on, my imagination went a little wild imagining exactly what Xander had done to Ryan.

I rambled around the empty apartment trying to find

things to occupy my mind, but my thoughts kept going back to our fight. For nearly two months I'd lived with him. I'd fallen in love with him. He claimed he'd fallen in love with me, too. But fundamentally, we were different. He would always try to solve my problems for me. Always want to ride in and save the day. *But maybe he has a point.* I tried to shove the thought out of my head, but it wouldn't go. I had been keeping him at arm's length. That way he couldn't disappoint me. *Like your father.*

But he didn't let me love him either. The whole thing was just so fucked up. He'd acted when I couldn't. He'd taken charge of his life, and mine. But I could see that he was still hurting. That his past still haunted him. After the things he'd told me last night, I should be worried. Should be sickened. Should be running in the opposite direction. But I didn't care. Alistair deserved to be strung up by his balls. Hell, I wished I'd been with those Russians when they'd gotten his location. I wanted to hurt him for what he'd helped do to Xander. Alistair might have just been a boy at the time, but that boy had grown into a man who'd deliberately tried to hurt him.

My phone chimed and I pulled it out of my bag. The text was from Abbie.

Abbie: *Great job last night. Do you want to go shopping today?*

I smiled. At least I'd made a friend out of this whole

mess. Maybe I didn't have to feel alone, didn't have to be on my own.

Imani: *Do you mind if I come over instead? I'm looking for something low-key.*

The response was quick.

Abbie: *Sure thing. Come over any time. I'm in Chiswick today.*

After a shower and a quick train ride, I walked along the cobblestones and past the mansions to Abbie and Faith's place. Chiswick was full of multi-million-dollar mansions perched right next to regular homes and flats. When I arrived, Abbie swung the door open with a grin. "What's happening, theater star?"

I laughed. "Hardly. I'll settle for working actress."

"Yeah, but not as fun to say. Come on in."

"You and Faith just hanging?"

Abbie laughed. "Let's just say Faith is sleeping off some of her overindulgence from last night. Max and Sophie are in Scotland for the day. I think he's looking at new property. Not that she's here that often anyway. I wonder why she just doesn't give up and say she lives with him."

Abbie led the way through the darkened foyer and eyed me. "So, what's up? You seem quiet."

I shook my head. "I'm fine. I—"

Abbie's brows drew up. "You gonna bullshit me?"

I sighed. "I guess not. You've spoken to Xander?"

"Yeah. He was a real mess but didn't go into details." Abbie grabbed a couple of sodas and handed one to me. "Why don't you tell me what happened?"

I followed her into the living room. Once I sat down across from my friend, I unloaded every fear I'd had over the last several weeks and the play-by-play of our fight last night, leaving out the sex.

When I was done, Abbie sat back.

"Holy fuck."

"I know." I scrubbed a hand through my curls. "I don't need this right now. I've got another show tonight."

"And you need to focus on that."

"And what about Xander? I can't even deal with him right now. Even if I could, I don't know what I'm supposed to say to him. Maybe neither one of us is capable of love or being in a relationship."

Abbie blew out a breath. "I don't think that's the case. He's complicated. You have to remember that he has no idea how to have a relationship. None whatsoever. The one person he loved abandoned him when she saw a potential chink in the armor. I love him, but he's selfish by nature. He has no experience with how to deal with someone else's needs, but you're the first woman he's tried with in years. He's going to fuck up once in a while."

I sagged. "I know, but I can't believe it. He deliberately took away my ability to make my own decisions. After Ryan, that's something that is really important to me. Having it stripped from me feels shitty. I mean, I'm not an idiot. I know he flew in Ebony just for my show, and he wants to be there for me. I just don't want to end up in a situation where I have no say about what happens in my life."

"It is fucked up. And I wish I could apologize on his behalf. But you have to know he loves you. He just has no idea how to show you properly. Did you tell him what you told me just now?"

"Probably not very effectively."

We sat silently like that for several minutes. Finally, Abbie asked me, "What do you want to do?"

"What I want to do is run to him and hold him and forget all this other stuff, but I don't think I can do that. He took my choices away from me."

"You guys have to talk in order to work it out. You can't ignore it and make it go away."

I had some soul searching ahead of me. "I have a show to do. Then I'll figure it out." It was all I could manage for the time being.

"Imani, thanks for meeting me."

I squared my shoulders. The last thing I wanted to do was meet this asshole. But I needed to do this. Everything that happened between us that fateful night would forever control me if I didn't. "Ryan. Let's make this quick."

He flattened his lips. "Do you see what your boyfriend did to me?"

I refused to wince at the mention of Xander. This meeting wasn't about Xander. It was about *us*. It was about *me*. It was about something I should have taken care of years ago.

"Is that why you asked me here? To look at a black eye?"

"Two. That thug gave me *two* black eyes. I'm not going to work for a month thanks to him."

He deserved far worse. "Not my problem, Ryan. You did this to yourself. For starters, I wasn't there. I don't know who gave you those black eyes. And secondly, you likely deserved what you got."

"I'm going to sue him. But you can stop that from happening."

He really was a total slimeball. How had I ever even compared the two? While Xander was overbearing, he didn't really try to control who I was as a person. Ryan, on the other hand, only wanted to serve his own agenda. "You do whatever you think you need to do. But let me go ahead and tell you this; there is nothing I'm going to do to intervene."

"He has a lot of money, and he'll need to pay for what he did. But you can stop that. If you just sign some papers stating you'll never slander me, then we can be done with this whole mess. We'll never have to see each other or talk about it again."

I blinked at him in surprise. He looked completely self-assured about his request. It didn't matter what he'd said at the time about being sorry. All he cared about was covering his own ass. I rolled my shoulders and met his gaze levelly. "I can't do that, Ryan, especially since I'm pressing charges as soon as I leave here today."

The genial mask slipped, and he looked thunderous, his brows snapping down. "What the fuck are you talking about?"

"The best part about this country, Ryan, is the statute of limitations on rape never runs out. And you should probably know that your attempts to intimidate me, and now blackmail me, will be noted."

He took a step toward me, and I was so happy that I'd insisted on meeting at the coffee shop right next to the police station. "No one will believe you, you slag."

I shook my head. "It doesn't matter. I'll report it. And since you did it to me, I know you've done it to someone else who will likely come forward. I'll tell the truth, and you won't be able to hold it over my head any longer. Threatening to tell the world. You told Xander, and I didn't die."

"You'll ruin my career."

"Well, you tried to ruin my life, so I guess we're even."

He reached a hand out, and I avoided his touch. "Don't do this."

"I made a mistake believing you when you said you were sorry. I won't be listening to you again."

Just because I had strong words for him didn't mean I wasn't terrified. I knew that pounding fear. That sick, gripping knot in my gut, telling me that I was in danger, that I was in trouble, that I had miscalculated, that I had taken several wrong steps. But this was going to be okay. I was safe, and he looked scared.

And I'd lied just a bit. I'd already reported him that morning. The police would want to speak to him shortly.

I stared at him for a moment. For as long as we dated, there was always something about him that made me a little bit afraid. And now I saw that he *liked* making me afraid. I didn't get that at all, because I was making him afraid at that moment, and it had zero appeal for me.

I stepped away. "Don't contact me. Don't call me. If you ever mention my name to the press, I'll come for you. I never want to speak to you again. You and I are done."

I turned, with each step I took away from him taking me closer and closer to freedom. He had controlled me for too long, made me afraid for too long, made me doubt myself for too long. Not anymore. I was no longer going to be that girl he'd met. The woman I'd become was too strong for that. I walked past the police station, feeling a little bit safer, a little bit happier. With each step I took, I knew I had gained a little part of myself back. The part I thought I had lost. When I got past the police station and down to the row of shops, I peered into one of the clothing shops, but despite needing to take my mind off of everything, it wasn't the time to go shopping.

There was too much unsettled. Besides, I just wanted to get home. At the light, I waited impatiently. But as I began to cross, someone grabbed my arm, pulling me back. His lips were close to my ear. "You think we're done, bitch?"

I opened my mouth to scream, but his grip on my arm tightened. "Do you feel this?" Something was shoved into my back. It was small. God, he had a gun? Where the hell would Ryan have gotten a gun? We were in the UK, you can't carry a gun here.

He pulled me aside into the alley, just in the shadows so that people walking by didn't ever really look inside, too afraid to see the seedier side of London. Too afraid to see what lurks just behind the shadows in the dark.

No one could see us there.

Ryan leaned close. "You're such a cunt."

All I could do was stare at him with my heart racing and sweat cooling my skin in thin layers. I had miscalculated. I had thought I could be brave and strong and walk away. I'd forgotten who I was dealing with.

"You think because you're fucking Xander Chase that you don't belong to me? No one is going to believe you Imani. Go to the police. Walk right in."

He's trying to scare you. Take a deep breath. You're going to be fine, and people are going to believe you. You can do this.

I tilted up my chin. "I'm not afraid of you."

He leaned forward and put his hand on my throat, and uselessly, I tried to grab it with one of mine. Then he had *both* his hands on my throat. "I want to choke you right now. Nobody would hear you scream."

I remembered my mother's insistence that I take self-defense classes when I started high school. And in that moment, her words really resonated with me. *You never know, baby. People can be assholes.*

Internally, I smiled at her warning, and I knew she was right. People could be assholes. People like Ryan. I raised my right arm over my head like I'd been shown in self-defense class. I forced my body to turn and rotate, even though I was losing air, and then I brought my arm down hard over his hands and sent my elbow flying back into his face. Blood spurted everywhere.

"If you come near me again, you'll be dead." Instead of heading toward the tube, I headed back to the police station. And instead of walking in with someone who loved me, I'd be walking in by myself. But it was okay. I was getting used to standing on my own.

XANDER

She hadn't come back. I had stayed up the rest of the

night hoping she'd come home. Because that's what it was to me, *our home*. But she'd walked out the front door, and she hadn't come back.

I'd tried calling and texting, of course. I mostly just wanted to know she was safe. Who the fuck was I trying to kid? I wanted to call and beg her to come home.

I'd really fucked up this time. I knew it; I just had no idea how to fix it. Once I took care of some work in the morning, I went by her place in Kingston to see her, but she wasn't home. When Felix opened the door, taking out the rubbish, he looked none too pleased. "You fucked up, didn't you?"

I scrubbed a hand down my face. "Look, mate, I just want to make sure she's physically okay."

"In that case she's fine."

"Is she with you?" I jammed my hands into my back pockets.

"No, but she sent me a text earlier. What did you do, anyway?"

I shook my head. "Something I promised I wouldn't."

Imani's best friend narrowed his eyes. "You realize how hard trust is to come by for that girl, right?"

"I know, okay? If I could take it back, I would. And at the time, I honestly thought I was helping. But all I did was cock it up. And now I have no idea how to fix it."

"You need to let her work it out." Felix crossed his arms over his chest. "She'd already been through enough when you came along. I knew it was a mistake, her whole plan, but she wouldn't take money from me and, well, she's hard to dissuade when she makes up her mind."

"Yes, I've met her." I had no idea where to go now. What to do. All I knew was that the empty hole in my chest, the one I'd filled with Imani these past few weeks, it burned, and that hollow feeling was spreading through my whole body. "Can you do me a favor?"

"I'm not inclined to do you any favors, mate." The way he said that word, *mate,* made it abundantly clear we weren't friends. Would never be friends as long as I was in Imani's bad books. "If I had my way, Imani would be living at home. Not playing happy housewife with you."

"I know. Look, just tell her I'm sorry. I just want to talk."

After I left Imani's, I battled the central London traffic to the barge. I'd asked Alexi to meet me there. When I arrived, my brother was on the deck waiting for me with a Guinness.

I approached warily. "What's the matter?"

Alexi took a sip. "You tell me. All Abbie did was text me and tell me that you'd had a rough morning and to give you a pint when you arrived."

Abbie. There she was, still trying to take care of me. That meant Imani was with her. Or that she'd at least seen her.

"Yeah, she's right. I could use it."

Lex inclined his head. "You want to go inside and talk about it?"

I nodded and followed my brother into the barge's open interior. When the sliding doors were open, it had a great indoor-outdoor feel to it. It had cost Lex a fortune to have the exterior walls built of reinforced glass on weather-proofed tracks. When he opened the glass doors, it looked like he lived on a completely open boat; when he closed the doors, the heat stayed trapped inside. And the glass was frosted to give him a sense of privacy.

I wondered if he'd keep this place once he and Abbie got married. Lex didn't waste time. "Imani left?"

Hearing the words out loud made my heart squeeze, and I rubbed at the hollow part of my chest. Was it supposed to hurt this much? "Yeah, I fucked up."

Lex listened intently while I talked. When I was done talking, Alexi took the beer out of my hand and handed me a glass tumbler of something dark. "Screw that; it's only two in the afternoon, but you need a stronger drink than that."

"That's what I'm trying to tell you."

"So, you took over her life when she was adamant about doing things on her own, but you refused to let her help you? You realize you took away her choice."

"She's clearly better off without me."

"If you really believed that, you wouldn't be here."

"I'm fucked up, mate. You were right. The whole Alistair thing has been eating me up. I've been consumed by it, and it's shadowed my judgment. And the worst part is that I can't blame what I did to her on this other shit. That was just me being me."

Alexi nodded. "The good news, Xan, is that you're capable of change if you really want it. But first you have to believe that people are capable of *anything*. You don't have to be like this. You can take real steps to heal. But that's entirely up to you. I can't force you, cajole you, or bribe you. If you say you're fine, then you're fine. But we both know you're not fine. Alistair proved that. Just to best him and make his life hell, you proposed to a woman. Granted, she was probably the only sane choice you made in this whole thing. You can't promise not to meddle, because that's who you are. But she's also right. You were manipulative. You did it to control her like you need to control everything else. The problem is she's a human being. She can't be controlled."

I sank into Lex's couch and dropped my head into my hands. "I just want her back. I'd do anything to fix shit between us."

"Then maybe for once you need to take a serious stab at fixing the shit inside you."

18

XANDER

"Alexander, what do you think I can help you with today?"

I tried to calm the jitters rushing through my blood. It was the only way to describe it. I was torn and nervous, and I did not want to be there.

"Well, I lost just about everything I care about, so I can't really avoid this therapy stuff for much longer."

Dr. Kaufman nodded and just watched me carefully. Abbie was right. She wasn't your typical therapist. She was young and beautiful, but not so beautiful you didn't want to talk to her. But there was something so... modern about her.

"Well, my girlfriend left me."

Not exactly true.

"I see."

Be honest you twat. "Okay, if I'm being honest, I pushed her away and forced her to leave."

"Okay, why did you do that?"

I sighed. "Because she was always probing me to talk, to explore my feelings, and I'm never keen on that."

Her smile was refreshing. "I'm picking up on that."

"At least I'm here. I just don't know how to do this."

"Okay, why don't you tell me why you want her back? That seems as good a place as any to help get you talking."

That was the easy part. "She's bright. Funny. Beautiful. Smart. She's an incredible actress. And when she's on the stage, you cannot take your eyes off of her. She makes me laugh. She makes me want to keep her safe. She makes me want to be better than I am. She makes me want to take care of her. And I'm too selfish to care about anyone."

"That's interesting. Most selfish people aren't aware enough to know that they're selfish."

"Oh, I know I'm selfish. I make things about me all the time. You can ask my brother. He'll tell you."

Her lips quirked into a soft smile. "You're Alexi's brother, right? He and Abbie, they both gave the referral."

I nodded. "Yup. Of the two of us, he is the better man."

"That is the second time you have said that. Why do you think he's better?"

"Because he did what I couldn't. Because he let go when I couldn't. Because he is literally a better person. He's just as fucked up from our childhood as I was, but he didn't deliberately try and hurt anyone."

Her brows lifted. "Have you deliberately tried to hurt someone?"

"Not by my own hand, but by not caring what happens to them, yes."

She nodded. Still not writing anything down.

"Why don't you start at the beginning? Tell me about you and Alexi growing up. Then we'll move on from there."

I watched her. "My brother has already told you."

"Yes, but I need *you* to tell me."

"But why? He's already done the dirty work."

"Yes, but that was work for him. This is work for *you*, and I need you to actually do the work."

I frowned. "This isn't going to be easy, is it?"

"No. It's not. But that's kind of the point, isn't it? The work that you and I are going to explore will include things that are going to make you uncomfortable and probably sad. Things that are going to be difficult for you to talk about. But when you do, and you're looking out on the other side, you'll be a better person. Possibly understand yourself better, be able to connect with other people more. Isn't that what you want?"

I considered what my life had been like without Imani. Waking up without her. Trying to focus on things without her in my life, and I couldn't do it. "Yes. What do you need?"

"I need you to tell me about the events that brought you here. Tell me about your childhood, about your life. Tell me about who you are and who you want to be. I can't help you get there unless I know where you've been."

I ran my hands through my hair. "Do you mind if I pace?"

She gave a little laugh. "Sure. Walk around. Do whatever you need. But the key is, in here, we talk."

I scrubbed a hand over my jaw. I was mildly surprised at the stubble. When was the last time I'd shaved? "I spent my whole life *not* talking. When I need to feel something or express something, I usually take a photo. It makes it easier to channel."

"And you're a very talented photographer. Some of your photos are quite haunting."

"Thanks, doc. I didn't know you knew my work."

"Well, I do my research on my patients. But you're stalling."

Jesus, she wouldn't let anything slide.

And that's what you need.

"When my brother and I were kids, my mom had a fiancé. He was the worst kind of predator. The kind that presents a pretty picture to the world and then tortures you at night. And he'd groomed his son to help him. That's what's in my past."

She merely watched me silently, leaving me to talk more, willing me to open. Part of me wanted to suddenly refuse, but Christ, if I didn't talk about it, I wouldn't get her back.

And you can't live without her

I walked back to the couch across from her and forced myself to ease in. I squared my shoulders. When I opened my mouth, I let it all out.

From Silas to Alistair, to the drugs, the women, the booze, the whores, it all came pouring out. I told her about how I'd met Imani. How because of her, having sex hadn't felt like a waste of time and space. That because of her I could *feel* things. The problem with feeling things after not bothering for so long was that it hurt. But I told her all the things that I needed to let out. The things I'd been holding on to since I was a scared little boy hiding under the bed. Because the only way I was going to get back the woman I loved was if I was willing to bleed my soul for her. And before I could be the man she needed, I had to kill the man that I was.

And it was going to take a lot of blood.

19

I stared at the phone. Why the fuck was Garett calling me?

"Garett? What's the matter?"

"Mate, I know you said to keep an eye on the Ryan problem."

God, that git just wouldn't stay down.

"What's the matter?"

He took a breath before responding. "I need you to stay calm."

I sat up straighter. "If you want me to stay calm, spit it out."

"Imani met with him yesterday."

My heart raced. "What?" *Shit. Bugger. Fuck.*

"Did he hurt her? Did she go somewhere with him after?"

"No. She went to the police after they met, and then she got into a minicab. I can investigate where it took her if you want."

I ground my teeth. I'd promised I would give her space, but I needed to know if she was bloody okay, so when I couldn't find her, I put Garett on it for my own peace of mind, even though I knew she wouldn't want that. "Details."

"After the meeting with him, he tried to get handsy, followed her, and pulled her into an alley."

It was amazing how quickly the rage flickered to life, never far from the surface, never really gone, just slightly diminished. But it flared to life quickly like hot embers with just enough oxygen. "Where is he now?"

Garett sighed. "Xan, I'd follow you anywhere, but this is a fool's errand."

"Where the fuck is he?"

He rattled off the address, and I grabbed my jacket before he could even say the next thing. As I shoved at my elevator button, he talked quickly. "Police are already sitting on his residence. A restraining order has been served. She filed charges against him for yesterday's incident and for a previous assault."

Holy shit. She'd done it. She'd actually fucking done it. "Wow, okay. I'll be there in twenty."

"That's the thing Xander. You can't go at this dead-on. Word already broke to the news outlets. They've surrounded his place. You will be seen."

Fuck. "Jesus Christ."

"I'll keep an eye on him. If things die down, or if there is a way to get to him, I'll let you know."

I dragged my hands through my hair. I needed to fucking do something. *Anything.*

Maybe I needed to call the doc? None of this shit was healthy. *Fuck.* Who the fuck was I in this situation? Unable to help the woman I loved, one who currently wasn't speaking to me. And I couldn't do the one thing she needed.

She had gone to see him alone. Which was... How the hell could she do that?

She wasn't alone. She went to see him in public.

But the asshole followed her after. Had she learned nothing? Why hadn't she called me?

Not like you two are talking at the moment.

God, I didn't know what to do. I had no idea how to deal with any of it. After another thirty minutes of indecision, I did the one thing I didn't think I would ever do.

I called Dr. Kaufman. At first, her answering service picked up, and I was forced to leave a message. I wasn't used to believing in anything good happening, but within two minutes, she called. "Mr. Chase, I'm surprised to hear from you."

"Well, I think I'm about to do something stupid."

"I am impressed that you called me first. I have to warn you, if this something is illegal and you disclose it to me, and you haven't yet committed it, I will be forced to call the police."

"*Fuck.*"

"Why don't you walk me through what you're feeling at the moment?"

"I don't want to walk you through what I'm fucking *feeling.*"

"Then why did you call me, Xander?"

Bugger. "Okay, I'm feeling angry. Impotent. Furious."

"That's the same as angry."

"Really, semantics?"

"I'm just asking you to be specific."

"Fine. I'm confused. Hurt. Hopeless."

"Ah, there we go. What happened?"

Before I knew it, I was spilling my guts. I told her about how Imani went to meet Ryan... fucking alone. How the asshole had hurt her and how I wanted to fix the problem for her.

"But you can't fix the problem because the news outlets already have this and they're staking it out?"

"Yes."

"I want you to think through it. You are angry about the media not letting you have an outlet for your anger."

"Yes, why don't you see that?"

"I do see it. I just need *you* to see it."

I forced myself to take a deep breath. When that didn't really help to calm me down, I took another. And then another. When I was finally calm enough, I ground my teeth. "My anger won't solve anything."

"That's a good start. What else?"

"Imani doesn't want me running in to fix her problems."

"That's very good."

"See, doc? I can make progress." The problem with that statement was that I could still hear the anger in my voice.

"So, about the doing something illegal part?"

"No, I merely want to have a conversation with him."

"Will this conversation involve blood?"

I frowned. There were surely a million ways to hit him without him bleeding. "Not necessarily."

Her chuckle was low and soft. "Xander, while physically assaulting him will make you feel better in the short-term, will it fix anything with Imani?"

And there lay the rub. Imani wouldn't thank me for it. She would be pissed. She'd met with him. I had no idea why. But if I knew her at all, I suspected she was drawing her line in the sand. Refusing to be afraid of him anymore.

Given the details Garett had given me, she'd been smart. She'd done it near the police station. And then when he'd grabbed her, Imani had filed a report, a restraining order, and a warrant to have him arrested, which was exactly what she should have done.

Except, you weren't there to save her.

"She doesn't need me to save her."

I could almost hear Dr. Kaufman smile on the phone. "That's it, exactly. So, if you went after him, would that action be for her, or would that be for you?"

"Fuck. I hate you."

"You would not be my first patient to say that."

"Why do I feel like this? I'm not used to feeling everything all at once."

"Well, when you repress your emotions for so long, when they finally find their way out, they're hard to stop. But you did the right thing by calling me."

"You weren't exactly my first call."

She laughed again. "But you *did* call me just the same. Because if you were doing something illegal right now, there isn't anything I could do to help."

"Shit, so I should have done the thing and *then* called you?"

"No, Xander."

"I'm kidding. Jesus." I wasn't.

"How are you feeling now?"

I frowned as I stared down at my jacket in my hands. The elevator door had closed already, and I noticed my feet were bare. I'd been ready to walk out of the house in bare feet to fix the problem. But Imani had already fixed it on her own.

I wasn't a fan of these new emotions. "I feel deflated. I feel tired. I feel disappointed. I feel empty. Guilty. Sad."

"Excellent."

"You're happy I feel sad? What kind of quack are you?"

"No, I'm happy you're feeling something. You went through such a long period in your life trying not to feel that you got used to that numbness. And now you're letting new emotions out in a healthy way, not in a way that involves you doing things that are harmful to yourself or others."

"The itch is still there, doc."

"The itch to do harm or the itch to go out and have sex?"

I frowned because that secondary itch was there. But I knew whoever I slept with wouldn't be Imani, so I didn't want that.

"The itch to do harm. The itch for sex is like a constant hum. But it's for her. Not anyone else."

"Excellent, Xander. See, you're really working through it. You're already making progress."

"This is going to take a lot longer than I thought, isn't it?"

"Yeah, probably. But the good news is you're doing what you need to do. It'll happen when it happens."

When I finally hung up my call with the Dr. Kaufman, I turned around, hung my jacket back up, and texted Garett.

Xander: *If and when you find an opening for Ryan, don't tell me. Ever.*

Garett: *You got it.*

Xander: *Also, see if you can find Imani.*

Garett: *Already on it.*

I could do this. I could be a better person for her. But I had to let her know I was trying and that I was sorry for the way I'd behaved.

20

XANDER

None of this was a good idea. I knew that. But I needed to at least say I was sorry. Properly.

Unfortunately, Imani wasn't at the flat when I knocked.

Garett had worked out that she'd moved out from Fe's. Well, at least the building that he lived in, but he owned another place that was a block away. Smaller. Nondescript. The neighborhood was safe, though. The doormen were respectable but not overly posh. I behaved myself and didn't force my way past them, even though I knew they recognized me.

When she finally came home, she paused as she rounded the stairs. "Jesus Christ. Xander, what are you doing here? Are you okay?"

I stared down at my feet. If I looked at her for too long, I'd be so tempted to hold her. "Hey, I'm fine. I just — Can I talk to you for a minute?"

She hesitated for a moment and then motioned for me to follow her up the stairs. When we got to her new apartment, she unlocked the door, stepping aside to let me in.

The flat might be smaller than ours had been, but it was still homey. There were photos everywhere. Candles, throw pillows, and all those things that made a place a home. Made the place look lived in.

"What's up, Xander?"

"Listen, I—" There I was, finally talking to her, and I had no idea what to say.

"Do you want some tea?"

I shook my head. "No, I'm sorry. I didn't mean to intrude, I just— All of a sudden I have no idea what to say."

She tucked her hands in the back pockets of her jeans. "If it helps, neither do I."

"You don't have to say anything, Imani." And then suddenly the words were right there on the tip of my tongue. But the fear was trying to pull them back and hold them in.

I could almost feel Dr. Kaufman in the back of my

head, hacking away at the chains. Then finally, I could speak freely. "I know you don't want to see me. And honestly, I probably shouldn't be seeing you."

She frowned at that. "Okay, then what are you doing here?"

"Sorry, that didn't turn out right. What I mean is that I'm a broken disaster. And you were right to leave. I've never taken responsibility for anything. I am selfish. And a pain in the ass. Demanding. I want what I want when I want it. And every time an emotion should even bubble anywhere near the surface, I jam it down. Until you walked out, I didn't realize that I haven't cared about anything for most of my life, besides Lex, anyway. And photography. But even where that is concerned, I've been closed off a little too. The way I've handled my problems, shoving down the emotions and how I feel about them, wasn't right. And that was no way to connect to any kind of relationship."

She blinked rapidly, and I could see the shine in her eyes. I wanted to hold her tight. I didn't want to let her go, ever. But I held myself still. "I'm trying to fix some things about myself. I need a lot of work. But maybe if I do the work, and if you're still available when I'm done, maybe we can talk."

She sniffed, the tears falling freely now. "I would really like that."

I nodded. "That's all I wanted to say. I'm sorry I made you leave. We had so much—too much—between us. And none of that was going to make me better until one of us was brave enough to do something. So thank you for being braver than me. I should have respected your bravery instead of pushing you away."

"You are brave. I wish you could see how much."

I nodded. "I'm working on that, but there's a lot of work to be done."

"Isn't there always?"

I nodded. "So I'm going to get out of your hair. But um, just, you know, before I go..."

She nodded. "Yeah?"

"I heard about Ryan, and I'm so sorry."

Her eyes went wide. "How did you hear about Ryan?"

I should tell her the truth here, but we'd already made progress. "Let's just say I pay attention to what's happening in the news." *Coward.*

She blinked. "Jesus. You saw that?"

Be honest. No evasions. "And... I had Garett tailing him."

She laughed and shook her head. "Of course, you did. I guess you tailed him for me?"

I nodded. "Yeah. But I didn't do anything about it. I

didn't go see him. I didn't go beat him within an inch of his life."

She frowned. "Why not?"

"Trust me, I wanted to. But I knew you *wouldn't* want me to. And I have already tried to ride in on my white steed for you one too many times. But you have your own horse, and you are an excellent rider."

"Hell yes, I am."

"But I'm always ready to help you. Just in case, you know, you're wondering."

"Xander, you know I didn't let you push me away because I don't care about you."

I gave her a soft smile. "I know. If you had stayed, I would have destroyed you, and I would hate myself even more than I already do. So I'm going to do what I need to do, and you know, learn how to be the man you deserve."

Then I opened the door and walked out. I had to, because if she'd said the words that were in her eyes, I wouldn't have been able to go.

I would have stayed. I would have held her. I would have kissed her. I would have fucked her in all the ways I had dreamt of since she'd walked out. I would have made up for the lost time. I would have kept her in that bed, chained to me. I would have made it impossible for either one of us to think, to act, to stop. But that wasn't what either one of us needed right then.

There would be time for that. In the meantime, I was going to fix *me*, as much as I could anyway. I'd already taken steps toward that. And I had to admit, it felt good.

⚜

3 Months Later...

Xander

Things used to come easy for me. But none of those things mattered until I met Imani. For so long all I'd cared about was revenge, but now all I wanted was her.

I inhaled the dry New England air. It smelled different than in London. Late summer heralded a slight changing of leaves that I knew would be stunning. I'd done a shoot in Connecticut years ago. But I wasn't there for work. I was there for love.

I'd never been so nervous in my life, but I had to do this. If she still didn't want me, that was fair enough, but at least I'd given it my best shot.

It was Imani who answered the door. She yanked it open with a half-smile, which contorted to shock when she saw me. "X-Xander. Are you okay?"

I shook my head. "No. I'm not okay. I'm a ridiculously fucked-up mess, and the woman I love has been away from me for three long months. But I couldn't be without her anymore, and I was hoping she'd be willing to talk to me." I also wanted to kiss her desperately.

"Xander," she breathed.

"I've missed you. When Abbie told me you'd left, I couldn't believe it."

"I wanted to help Ebony pack and spend some quality time with Dad and help him out a little." She inclined her head toward the house. "I don't think I ever said thank you for what you did. He's been going to counseling. Stayed sober for three months." She shrugged. "It's a start."

"That's great, Imani. I'm happy to hear that."

I cleared my throat. I needed to say my piece so I could run back to the safety of my city. "I know I made a huge mistake with you. And I can't change it. My heart was in the right place, but it was wrong. I had no right to move you around the chessboard and treat you like a pawn. It's a bad habit, and I'm working on fixing it. I know I took away some of your strength, and I'm sorry for that." I cleared my throat and kicked at the welcome mat. "I, uh, also started therapy with Lex. It's been helping. I'm having fewer nightmares now."

She reached out her hand to me. "Oh, Xander."

I ached to have her touch me, but I understood she probably wouldn't want that. Her eyes shimmered, and it nearly broke my heart. "I just want to say that I love you. It was real for me in more ways than I ever knew could be possible. For the first time, I cared about someone besides Lex, and I liked it. You challenged me and made me mad. You were in my space, and I loved every minute of it. From the moment you asked if I was singularly an asshole or not, it's been impossible for me to get you out of my head. I love you so completely, and I'm sorry I hurt you. It was never my intention."

"Xander."

"Sorry, if you could just let me finish. I only want to give you what you want, but if you saw fit to give me another—"

She interrupted me with a kiss, wrapping her arms around my neck and squeezing tight. The blood rushed in my head. She tasted of apples and cinnamon and her. I sank into it, holding her tight, not daring to believe this was real.

When she pulled back, I was reluctant to let her go. She licked her lips. "I missed you. I'm so sorry. I just needed some time to think, where everything about my life wasn't consumed by you. I was coming back in a few weeks, and you were my first planned stop. I was a little worried you might have moved on."

Moved on? Was she mad? "I dream about you every night."

"Xander?"

"Yeah?" My heart dared to hope, and I stood perfectly still.

"I love you."

All the tension rolled off my shoulders and I breathed a deep sigh of relief. "I love you too. And I plan on spending a lot of time showing you just how much."

F*our Years Later…*
The first thing I felt was pain. My head hurt. Everything hurt, and something was in my throat. I couldn't swallow. Hard plastic. I started to cough, and there was a beeping sound. So loud. Why? Why was it so loud? And then something was dragging me down, holding my arms. I couldn't move. I couldn't open my eyes. Jesus Christ. *Oh my God, my baby. Xander.*

The accident.

"Mrs. Chase. Mrs. Chase, we need you to calm down. We're going to remove the intubation, and then we'll take the bandages off your eyes."

Bandages?

Another voice, a deeper one, said, "You don't have to

do that. Don't hold her down. She won't like it. You're just scaring her."

Xander. He is here. Is he okay?

And then the plastic tube was removed, making me gag. Ugh, my stomach was swirling, and it hurt. But then the tube was gone, and I could breathe. Oh God, I had to suck to get air, and it smelled like Lysol had been sprayed all over the room.

I tried to raise my hands to my eyes to remove whatever it was that was making it so dark.

I tried to lift my arms again, but someone once again held me down.

"I told you to stop that."

I could move, but oh God, it hurt.

"Easy intern. I'll do it."

When the gauze was finally out of the way, it was so bright in the room that I blinked several times and then squinted, my gaze searching for Xander.

I didn't have to look far. He was right on my left. "Hi."

His smile was tremulous. And he had stubble, well on its way to a beard.

"You haven't shaved." My voice sounded raspy to my own ears.

He chuckled low. "Leave it to my wife to complain

about beard burn. It's the first thing she does when she wakes."

I smiled. "Beard burn can be fun."

He laughed and then dropped his head. I could have sworn there was another chuckle on my right. Maybe two?

There were other people there? I tried to turn my head and winced. "It hurts."

Xander's voice was soft. "Yeah, it's going to hurt. You need to take it easy, love. You can't do too much too soon. The fact that you're awake and talking, that's a great sign, and I'm so proud of you."

I frowned. "Why would you be proud of me? Being awake and talking is hardly something special. Why does everything hurt?"

Oh God, the baby. My hands moved to my belly, but it was smaller than I was used to. Frantically, I tried to grab at the sheets. This time, Xander took my hands. "Imani, look at me love."

"Blueberry, where is she? What happened?"

Tears were streaming from my eyes, but I wasn't even aware that I was crying until he brushed them away. "She's all right. She's just in an incubator. They had to do an emergency C-section, okay? But she's perfectly fine. She's small, but she's a fighter. Such a fighter like her mum."

"She's here already?"

He nodded. "For eight days now."

"Eight days? Jesus, how long was I out? Is she—" I couldn't bear to ask. I remembered the accident. There had been a car accident, so if they had to do an emergency C-section, then... "I-is she really okay?"

His smile was tremulous. His dark hair fell over his brow as he took my hand and kissed my knuckles. "She's perfect. She's got a set of lungs on her, so that's good. She just needs a little more cooking to get bigger. But when it's time to feed her, she makes sure everyone knows it."

"Feed her? How—how are you feeding her?"

The nurse stepped forward on my right. "You've been out for several days, so you obviously haven't been able to nurse. But now that your injuries are healing, we can go ahead and give nursing a try. It takes a few days for your milk to come in anyway."

I frowned. "I missed so much of her life already."

Xander held on to my hand. "It's okay. It's okay. You needed to heal, and she needed to grow a little. I handled it while you rested. I told you I was going to be here on time for duty."

"I want to see her." I tried to get out of the bed, but that set off screeching beeps everywhere, and no less than three people rushed forward to stop me from trying to do such a crazy thing.

The nurse on my right tsked. "No, Mrs. Chase. You have a concussion. You have lacerations on your arm and your face, one right above your eye, so we bandaged it. Your eyes have been so swollen, you couldn't see. You've had a C-section, after which we normally would get you out of bed right away to start walking, but you also have several broken ribs and your spleen ruptured."

I cursed under my breath. "Jesus Christ."

Xander nodded. "You are a mess. But you're going to be better. Soon. And Kaya is here."

"I'm sad you've met her already and I haven't. I want to see her."

"They're having her brought in. I promise."

"Xander, I'm scared. What if something I did—"

He shook his head vehemently. "You didn't do anything wrong. Those fuckers shot at you. At us. They tried to take away my family. I will ruin them. I swear to God, if it's the last thing I'd do, I will ruin them."

I frowned. "Xander, I don't want any of that. I don't want you going down that deep dark hole again."

He frowned. "This isn't like Alistair. I swear to God. But you could have died. And they did that to you."

"I know, but I just want my family. I want to hold my baby, and hold you, and for us to have a life together. If you do this, it will take you right down into the dark."

"I won't be in the dark. I'm not leaving your side."

He might not be leaving my side, but he had full-on vengeance on his mind. "Xander, promise me you're not going to do anything to jeopardize your life."

He hung his head. "I think I already have."

I frowned. "What do you mean?"

"This all happened because I told my mother that I'd be her successor. She announced it to all her advisors. One of them likely had someone who followed us. Someone working with our cousin."

"You think it's because of some royal conspiracy that they shot at us?"

"Yeah, Imani, someone definitely shot at us. I just need to know who."

"I see the look on your face, Xan. It's not your fault."

"Of course, it is. I endangered your life because of ego and because I wanted to prove everyone wrong. They told me my whole life that I could be a prince, but I couldn't be the successor."

"This isn't your fault. You didn't lead them to do this. Put the blame where it lies. You're not going down into that dark world again, Xander."

I coughed, and the nurse was right back at my side. "She's had enough for now, Mr. Chase."

He squeezed my hand. "Listen, you rest. You're awake now, and we have all the time in the world to talk about this. I promise. I love you. But first, why don't you meet our baby?"

The nurses brought a little pink bundle in a clear bassinet. One of the nurses reached in and scooped her up with a smile on her face, and she made these little cooing noises.

Oh my God, that was my daughter.

Then they handed her to me. She blinked her little eyes at me and waved an angry fist in the air. Then she cooed and promptly went back to sleep.

"Oh my God, she's gorgeous."

Xander gave me a wide smile. "Yeah, of course, she is. She looks just like her mother."

"I love you."

"I love you with all of my breath. I promise you I will protect our family."

I knew he would. My only concern was exactly what he'd do to make sure he kept that promise.

"You know, when you needed somewhere for your little clubhouse, I didn't know we'd have royalty. I would have spruced up the place."

I watched as Roone's cousin, Ben Covington, sauntered in and said hi to everyone. I'd met him briefly at Roone and Jessa's wedding, but we hadn't had much time to talk.

He met my gaze and nodded. "I'm sorry for what happened to you, Xander. Any help the London Lords can give you, it's yours."

I nodded my thanks. I couldn't be trusted to talk at the moment. Everything was still too raw, too much. It was funny, because Alexi moved next to me like my shadow, ever watchful and making sure I wouldn't fly off the handle and go off the reservation, whatever it was. It was reassuring. I just wanted to get this over with so I could get back to the hospital to Imani and Kaya.

I still didn't believe everyone would come. I didn't even know who some of them were. They were my family, but when I put out the call, I hadn't expected *all* of the Winston Isles to come *en massse*. Sebastian was there, obviously, with Penny in tow. Their daughter played in their lap. I appreciated that they came, but I hadn't expected it.

Lucas was there. His fiancée, Bryna, was in his lap. I did wonder when he was going to marry her. They'd been engaged for a while, but I knew better than to call him out and ask. That would have just been cruel. Nothing like an impatient fiancée to make a bloke's life hell.

And Roone. The princess was on her feet behind him, looking every bit the warrior she was. Prince Tristan was in attendance, looking all sorts of uncomfortable. And Ben was there. He'd brought along his two partners, East and Bridge.

The whole room was like bloody men's fashion week had come to town. It was one good-looking family. In the far corner, with the Blake Security squad, was none other than Noah Blake himself and Matthias Weller. Mathias's wife was also there, looking every bit the badass. Dark hair flowing, gaze assessing everything.

I stepped forward. "I appreciate all of you coming at

my request. I didn't expect everyone to just drop what they were doing on such short notice."

Sebastian gave me an answering nod. "You don't have to thank us. This is Imani, she's family. Of course, we were going to come."

Nevertheless, I gave him a nod of appreciation. They'd all come, but Jesus...

"Look, this is primarily a security issue. As most of you know, someone attacked after it was announced that my uncle had been assassinated and my mother became the de facto heir to the throne of Nomea. She hasn't made her official announcement of acceptance yet, nor has she publicly named her successor. But before the incident, Alexi officially stepped aside, and I have fallen on the sword, so to speak. Not two hours later, we were attacked on the way home."

Everybody cursed under their breath, some more inventively than others. "I appreciate the sentiment. I didn't expect all of you to turn out for this, but I did ask Sebastian to help me find the people responsible. I would have handled it myself, but obviously, I've been occupied at the hospital with the baby and Imani. So, Sebastian, any help you and your team can give me will be much appreciated.

Sebastian nodded. "We've got Blake Security on the task in terms of finding them. As you know, we've dealt with our share of conspiracies and plots against the throne of the Winston Isles as well. We can find them, but the question is, what do you want us to do beyond that?"

I met my cousin's gaze levelly. "You let me worry about that."

Penny frowned and stepped forward. "Xander, what do you plan to do with them?"

I leveled a gaze on her. "And I told you not to worry about that. I just need help finding them."

Sebastian lifted a brow. "Xander, you're angry. You want someone to pay."

"Too right, I do. My daughter has been in an incubator without her mother for more than a week because of those bastards. So let's not stand here and try and explain to me how this is going to go. Besides, you're not my king."

The muscle in my cousin's jaw ticked. When he spoke, his voice was even in measure. "I get that. I know all about the anger coursing through your veins. I also know that anger won't get the job done. If you do find them, then what? You're going to kill someone?"

I tilted my chin up, but I said nothing.

Lucas spoke up then. "Look, I'm here for moral ambiguity and whatnot, but I'm more a thief than a murderer."

Half the people in the room shouted back at him, "Former thief."

Ben was the only one who grinned at him. Lucas grinned back. I watched as Ben tapped his wrist and Lucas looked on his hand and then scowled at Ben as he held out the watch.

Well, that was interesting. Good information to file away for later.

"Sebastian, either you're here to help, or you're not. If you're here to help, then you have to understand that I need to deal with this in my own way."

My cousin Derrick pushed to his feet. "As someone who has occasionally tripped down the shitty-morals rabbit-hole, I can testify that this is something you don't come back from."

"I understand and I hear you; I just don't care."

He nodded. "Fair enough. I'm all for finding and taking care of these assholes because they won't just be coming for you. If it's people who want the throne of Nomea, they'll come for all of us. Me, Theo, and Zia included."

Derrick's twin brother was off on his honeymoon, so I hadn't bothered to call him in. Although, knowing Theo's wife, she would have been all for operation *Let's Murder These Fuckers*. The door opened, and in strolled

Ariel with a squealing baby in her arms. "Oh, come on, Cash, you've got to give Auntie a break."

All eyes turned to her.

She stopped walking and cooed at the baby. "Oh, all right then. So, who are we going to kill, and when do we leave?"

I grinned at her and then turned my attention back to Sebastian. His eyes had softened as he watched his daughter looking so damn cute. She had a head full of dark curls, olive skin, two little teeth on the bottom, and was clearly displeased about something. As kids went, she was very cute. Penny rushed over and took her out of Ariel's arms. "Oh, Cash, give mommy a break."

Ariel grinned at the baby. "She's cute, but she's ornery and stubborn like her father." The two friends grinned at each other. Then Ariel swung her gaze back to me. "Seriously, who do we kill?"

Prince Tristan rolled his eyes. "Ariel, love, we try not to kill people, generally."

She just scoffed and ignored him. "No, seriously, someone came for one of ours, so we kill them. I feel like it's enough cause for murder. Eye for an eye and all that. Why are you staring at me like I'm the crazy person?"

I nodded in her direction. "I'm with you on the kill-them plan."

Matthias, in the corner, raised his hand. "I'm with you, too."

Next to him, his boss, Noah Blake, grabbed his arm and tugged it down. "He's *not* with you. We're not killing anyone."

Matthias sighed. "Sorry, I misspoke. I meant *have an aggressive* conversation. Sometimes murder just happens as a result."

Noah chuckled but still shook his head. "Look, we'll find who did this, and we'll bring them to justice. But no one is killing anyone. Unless, of course, they make a direct attempt on you, then these things happen."

I grinned then. "Yes, these things do indeed happen."

Next to me, I could feel Lex tensing. He didn't like the way the conversation was going.

"Look, just find who did this for me, and let's get this done. I need to get back to the hospital."

Ben stepped forward then. "Look, I understand vengeance, so I'll give you what you need. But from what I know of vengeance, you need to be sure it's what you want. Otherwise, it will cloud all your judgment, and any decisions made in a blind fog of rage, will be tainted. You need mental fucking clarity. When you have that, and only then, can we move forward."

I shot a pointed stare his way. "Thanks for those wise words. But are you in or not?"

He shrugged. "Oh, I'm in. If someone is getting their just desserts, I'm here for that."

I nodded. "Anyone else *not* in?"

Everyone looked uncomfortable, but not a single person stood down. They were all ready to follow me, ready to do what we needed to do. It wasn't just me and Lex anymore. We had a whole support system. A whole network of family backing us up. We were going to find those people who'd hurt my wife, and we were all going to make them pay.

23

IMANI

"What are you doing?"

I winced. I knew Xander wasn't going to be happy about seeing me up and about, but I could only stay confined to bed for so long, and the movement was good for my physical therapy. They'd let me leave the hospital the day before, providing I took it easy and made sure to get up and walk around on occasion. Xander didn't quite understand that, so he'd made sure all the staff knew I wasn't to be walking around. Thankfully, no one listened to him.

"I was just coming back from the bathroom," I lied. "I am still allowed to go to the bathroom, aren't I?"

He winced. "Imani, you're supposed to be resting."

"I'm also supposed to get exercise. Otherwise I won't heal right."

"You've only been home for a couple of days, and Kaya still isn't back from the hospital."

"I know. And I know we'll go see her tonight." I left out the part about when it was safer. "But honestly, Xander, this is too much. You can't hover and stop me from doing what I need to do too."

He scowled at me. "The usual way I would resolve this argument isn't really a viable option, and I don't want to yell at you."

"We're not having an argument, sweetheart. We're having a discussion about how you're too overprotective."

"You're mine to protect. How is that being overprotective?"

I rolled my eyes. "You know what, it's not like I'm going to die. Relax." His face drew to a frown immediately. "Jesus, I'm joking. I'm not going to die. We both know you'll go first because I have killed you in your sleep."

"Please God, let that be the way."

"I don't mean with sex."

Still, his lips twitched, and it was nice to see him do something other than scowl.

"Look, I'm okay. Most of my incisions and stitches are already healing. They said I'll be back in fighting shape in a couple of weeks, and I'm trying to make it half that amount. I missed a lot of time with Kaya while I was sleeping."

"Will you just stop and rest?"

"If you talk about rest one more time, I swear to God, I will kill you with my bare hands."

He lifted a brow. "Rest."

"Oh, you have jokes now? You're teasing me because you know I can't chase you."

"You actually have a good point... Then you're not ready."

I might not be ready, but the pillow was within reach. And so, I grabbed it and tossed it at him, wincing only a little as my side twinged.

"Imani, I swear to God."

"What are you going to do, hit me back?"

I could see the muscle ticking in his jaw. He either really wanted to laugh, or he really wanted to strangle me. Neither of which was actually going to take place. "Babe, I'm okay. You're going to have to let me out of your sight at some point."

"I have let you out of my sight. I had a job today, and I went to it."

"And let me guess, you were screaming the place down and made Abbie chase after you apologizing for your behavior."

He scowled. "I was not screaming the place down. It's

not my fault they had no idea how to take a good photograph."

"Sweetheart, we're both spending our mornings at the hospital with Kaya, and then we take a break and we go back in the evenings. You try to do too much, watching over me and Kaya and keeping us safe. You're going to crack if you don't talk to someone."

"I don't need to talk to anyone."

I crossed my arms and gave him the angry-wife-scowl number five. "Oh, really?"

"Yes, really. I'm fine."

"So, you're telling me there wasn't a secret meeting about finding out who shot at us and then killing them?"

"Jesus Christ, my fucking brother..."

I blinked several times. "Alexi was there? That jackass. He didn't tell me anything. Penny did."

His brows shot up. "Is nothing sacred?"

I laughed. "No, nothing is sacred. Especially if one's wife worries. What is wrong with you?"

"My cousin's people tried to take out my wife and unborn child. That deserves retaliation."

"I know that's how you think you feel, and probably it's not for me to tell you you're not angry, because of course, you are. But you're also scared. You're *mostly* scared. Now what happens with all that anger and fear if you find them and kill them? You're still going to be holding on to so much of that. Or you could talk to someone. Address those feelings and what they mean and how you need to deal with them."

"They don't mean anything. Of course, I'm doing great. Someone almost killed you."

"Yes, I'm well aware of that. They shoot like boys."

He frowned. "Like boys?"

"Well, most people say if someone's a bad shot they shoot like a girl. But I happen to know Penny's an excellent shot. As is Ariel. So they shoot like boys."

He chuckled then. "Fair enough, they shoot like boys."

I laughed. "They really should get a better aim. Besides, I'm a hard target."

He sighed. "Please, can you stop talking about this now?"

"Too soon?"

"Jesus Christ, too fucking soon."

"Fine. Fine. Tell me you're not going to do this."

"Sorry. I love you, but I can't."

"Xander, do you remember how you felt after Alistair? How worried you were that you'd actually almost been the agent of someone's death? It didn't sit well."

He ground his teeth. "But I could get over it this time. Put the feelings aside. I can feel okay with it."

"No, you wouldn't. Look, if you don't believe me, call Dr. Kaufman. When was the last time you saw her?"

He shrugged. "It's been a couple of years."

I nodded slowly. "Okay, then maybe it's time for a refresher of who you are now, Xander. What you're capable of and how it's going to make you feel."

He shook his head. "I don't want to. I want revenge. I want payback."

"I know. That's anger and fear talking. Kaya and I don't need angry, fearful Xander. We need whole Xander. The one who is in touch with his humanity. You're not capable of that kind of retribution anymore."

"Are you sure? The way I feel right now, I wouldn't bet on that if I were you."

That's not really what terrified me. As much as I loved him, there was a part of him that always thought he didn't deserve that love. And I worried that I would lose him to that part if we weren't careful.

24

XANDER

"You're sure you want to do this?"

I raised a brow. "I'm hiring you and your men, so don't let me down. And I want them brought to me. I will deal with them and send them back to Nomea in pieces."

Randall Brash, a contact I'd gotten from Garett, studied me closely. "And if they resist being removed?"

"I want you to make them *not* resist."

He nodded slowly. "I gotcha, boss."

"I certainly hope you do."

He nodded. "I know that Arron Slough, your cousin several times removed, would've been next in line. Had your mother not been available, he would have been the one. So likely, he and his boys are behind this. And he's a nasty bit of work. He's been to jail before. While he was abroad. Usually for charges like aggravated assault. But his friends, those he likes to roll with... Unsavory doesn't even begin to cover it. Drugs, violent crimes. So he or one of his crew is likely your guy."

I crossed my arms as I watched Randall. To any onlookers, we were merely standing outside, perhaps for a smoke. Randall laid out most of the plan, complete with maps, on the hood of my Bugatti. "It should be fairly simple. No muss, no fuss. We'll be in and out. Pick 'em up, and bring 'em here?"

I shook my head. "No. I don't want them anywhere near my family." I gave him the address to my Notting Hill flat. I never used it for anything anymore. But it seemed like a great place to temporarily house assholes while I dissuaded them of their plans to kill me and my family.

"Excellent. We'll leave tonight."

"Surveil first. I want the pickup clean. No trace back to me, my mother, or my brother. *Especially* my brother."

He nodded. "No one will know. It'll be fine. If you want, you can come with us to have a look. As soon as I have a location, I'll let you know."

"Thank you."

I turned and then startled to a stop. Behind me, my brother and my cousin were standing there blocking the way to the stairs back up to the townhouse, and both of them had their arms crossed and were shaking their heads. Alexi spoke first. "And here I thought if there was a call to rally and kill everyone, I would at least have been the first on your call list."

I sighed. "Alexi, let's not do this." I rubbed the back of my neck. "You and I both know full well, you're not killing anyone."

"Neither are you."

Sebastian just shrugged. "I mean, I'm here for killing period. But you didn't even call us. You didn't let us handle this like a team."

"I already told you, this is my headache."

Alexi shook his head. "At the very least, it's *our* headache. Yes, they got to you, but it's *our* mother on the throne. Let's not forget that."

I shuffled on my feet. I knew he'd see it like that. But couldn't he see I was trying to protect him? "Lex, be reasonable. You've already abdicated. They have no reason to go after you. It's me and Imani and Kaya who are in trouble."

"Yeah, but when are you going to understand that they are *my* family too?"

Sebastian added, "And you guys are my cousins. That's how we roll on Team Winston Isles."

I laughed. "Team Winston Isles, huh?"

"Yep. You were there for some of the whole Theo-

Derrick drama, so you're on that team. You know we do things together."

Lex nodded. "So, we're not letting you do this, at least not alone. If you insist on doing it, we're doing it with you."

"You idiot. Why can't you see that this is for the best?"

From behind me, Randall waved an arm. "Hey, boss, are we doing this, or are we not doing this?"

"We're doing it," I said at the same time Lex and Sebastian said, "We're not doing this."

I countered, "This is the only way to protect them."

Lex shook his head. "I know you *think* that. But there are other ways. We'll figure out something else."

Sebastian watched me closely. "I know that you think you have to fix everything. And I get that. I have the same problem. But sooner or later, you're going to learn that you're not alone. At the very least, you have Imani. She's yours. She's your heart. And after Imani, you have Kaya. And after them, you have Lex and Abbie, and me and Penny, and Lucas, Jessa, Roone, Tristan, and Ariel. You have the whole team. You are not an island anymore, Xander."

I swallowed hard around a lump in my throat. "They tried to take my family."

"I know." Sebastian nodded solemnly. "And God

forbid something *had* happened to them, the culprits would be dealt with in a very specific manner. And we *will* retaliate. There *will* be vengeance. But we're not going to get it by killing people. It's not what Imani wants."

I scowled. "Ugh, low blow. She doesn't need to know anything about this."

Lex laughed. "You really think your wife knows nothing about this? Look up."

I looked up and saw her waving from the window as she held Kaya in her arms. "Oh, fuck. You told her?"

Lex shrugged. "That you were trying to do this all on your own? Yeah. What do you think, I'm an idiot?"

I called back to Randall. "Yeah, plan's off for now."

He shrugged. "Whatever. Your money. Whenever you're ready, let me know."

"Will do." I turned back to my brother and cousin with a scowl. "You fucking involved my wife?"

Sebastian smiled. "I pull no punches. When I want something, I make it happen. Besides, I needed to remind you that you're not alone. That there is a better way to handle this situation, and it's as a team. Like it or not."

I sighed and looked up at the most beautiful woman in the world holding my baby. I knew what she'd say. That no matter what we did, it would be as a team. And as much as I tried to shield her from any of it, she wouldn't have it.

She was probably pissed I'd tried to do this on my own without telling her.

"How mad is she?"

Lex laughed. "Oh, you are in a mess of trouble. And for once, because she just had a baby and, you know, someone tried to kill her, you won't be able to use sex to get out of it. I can't wait until she hands you your ass."

"Some brother you are."

"Yeah, well, next time don't try and run a crusade without me. We'll find a solution, and we'll get there together. Like always."

He put out an arm, and I clasped it. He dragged me to him and held tight. It was the first real hug we'd had in a while, and that sure made my eyes sting. When I stepped back, I shoved him a little. "You recognize I'm supposed to be the older brother, right?"

"Yeah. Now start making decisions like you are."

I jumped when the trunk of the car behind me opened and out climbed Penny. "What the—"

"Oh my God. I was getting tired in there. It's hot tonight. So glad you decided not to go. But if you *were* going, I was coming with."

My eyes bugged. "Are you kidding me right now?"

"Nope."

Sebastian just shook his head. "Love, in the trunk?"

"What? I knew what he was going to try and do. I'm not dumb."

Across the street, the door to an SUV pushed open and out jumped Ariel and Jessa. "Penny, same idea?"

She waved at the others. "Yeah. The women in the Winston Isles don't fuck around."

Ariel rolled her eyes. "The men were all late."

They laughed at my expense, and I just glowered at them. "Oh my God, the whole lot of you are nutters."

My brother grinned. "Crazy possibly, but we are family, aren't we?"

He was right. We were doing this together or not at all.

EPILOGUE

I mani
Something was happening, but Xander wouldn't tell me what.

I was still pretty angry with him for trying to resolve everything on his own. How many times did I have to tell him that we were a unit? And now we had Kaya, our beautiful, perfect daughter with my smile and her father's eyes. He couldn't just run off and try and solve everything.

Next to me, he squeezed my hand. "You still mad?"

I slid him a glance. "Define mad, exactly."

"Have I told you how sexy you are when you're angry?"

"Xander, now is not the time."

He just grinned. The doctor had said that I

couldn't have sex for eight weeks, given the emergency cesarean. Xander had made a countdown clock, and the fool had found a way around that order. He was really very, very good with his mouth and hands. I'd like to say I didn't cut him any slack for being a complete idiot. But God, he had an amazing tongue. You could forgive anything for that tongue.

"It's your mother's coronation. She's about to announce a successor, and you're sitting here talking about how sexy I am? There are royals everywhere. You're supposed to show decorum."

He shrugged. "I don't really believe in decorum."

"Oh my God. Why do I have the feeling that you on the throne is going to be a terrifying prospect?"

He grinned. "Because I'm unpredictable?"

"And a giant pain in the—"

He grinned. "Go on, finish that line."

"I will not. It'll give you too much satisfaction," I huffed.

"You know I love talking about your ass. And I also love holding your ass. Squeezing it, spanking it."

"Xander. Keep your voice down."

I glanced around to make sure no one had heard him. To his right sat Lex and Abbie, and next to them were Penny and Sebastian, who held his son on his lap. The baby prince was chewing on what looked like a block of some sort.

Behind us were Roone, Jessa, Ariel and Tristan, and behind them were Derek, Theo and Zia. Also, Queen Mother Alexa. It was great to know that we had so much support. Across the aisle sat Xander's distant cousins, other relatives, and members of the royal court. Some members of the contingent I'd seen in the morning were missing though. Probably running late.

And then of course there was the press. So much press. Not that I really thought anyone was listening to our conversation, but if he was going to be prince, possibly king one day, he really was going to have to learn to follow some rules. Any rules. But as usual, he wasn't really down for listening to anyone but himself.

That's not true. He listens to you.

He did… but only when it suited him.

"Come on, no one's listening. We can talk about sex all we want and about exactly what I'm going to do to you the moment I slide my dick inside you."

"Xander!"

"You know you're missing me."

"You are such a pain. Keep it down."

"What? You think a king doesn't tell his queen how much he loves her and how much he wants her, and what he wants to do to her?"

"I just think maybe not so graphically or where everyone can hear."

He laughed. "But when would I tell you? Besides, I want everyone to hear. You are mine."

I just shook my head. "See, your complete shamelessness is how we ended up with this one."

In my arms, Kaya snuffled in her blanket, all warm and cozy, little mouth gently sucking on her tongue. She was happily sleeping through her father's outrageousness.

"Yeah, and she's the most perfect thing I've ever done in my life, so obviously, my shamelessness works."

I could only shake my head.

Everyone was summoned to attention by the head of the Council of Nomea. Some lord or something. Lord Winchester? I couldn't remember the name. I'd met a lot of lords and princes over the last few days. We still had heavy security, and Xander basically wouldn't let Kaya or me out of his sight, especially once Blake Security had been sent home after they finished fully training our permanent security detail.

"All rise."

We did, just as if we were in court. Then out came Xander's mother, dressed all in white. She looked resplendent. She wore a pantsuit with some kind of cape, looking to be part fairy and part businesswoman. I dug it and wondered if I could get away with that kind of look.

She stood at the podium and smiled down at all of us. "Ladies and gentlemen, lords, ladies, princes and princesses, kings and queens, and members of the royal court, I address you as the newly coronated Queen of Nomea. I want to thank you all for being here and showing your support for the return of my family from exile. I will strive to be a good ruler, fair and just and kind. My one and only goal will be to enrich and advance our people. To look after them, to wrap my arms around us all in the warm bosom of a mother, to teach our young, to encourage our dreamers. And this is my promise to you."

I smiled at Xander, and he was beaming up at his mother. "She looks like she was born for this."

He nodded. "She *was* born for this."

His mother continued. "I know many of you have wondered who will succeed me. I know there has been much speculation, and I have come to a decision, one that has been long and difficult but well thought out." I took Xander's hand and squeezed. He patted mine and then leaned over and kissed me on the forehead. Next to Xander, Alexi kept his eyes forward. I knew it wouldn't be Lex. He'd already abdicated. He didn't want to be king. That was why Xander had stepped up. I just prayed he knew what he was doing.

"I am pleased to announce that my successor to the throne will be Derrick Arlington."

My jaw unhinged. "What?" I turned to Xander, who looked not surprised at all.

"Yeah. That meeting I had with my mother?"

"You abdicated?"

He nodded. "Sure did."

I wasn't the only one surprised. Across the aisle, several of Xander's cousins' brows were raised and their mouths were open. There was a lot of head shaking going on. I turned around to look at Derrick, and he grinned at me and waved at a now-awake Kaya. All the murmuring had woken her. "You?" I asked.

He nodded and shrugged. "I feel like I could be a good king."

Next to him, his twin brother Theo rolled his eyes as he kissed his wife Zia's hand. "God help us all."

Derek chuckled and leaned over to his brother. "Don't worry. If you kill me, you can be king."

Watching the two of them exchange words really set it in stone for me. Xander was *free*. He wasn't going to be king. No one was going to scrutinize our lives. Kaya would be safe. But his legacy…

Behind us, the members of the press were on their feet. They were shouting questions, many of them waving enthusiastically and trying to get the queen's attention.

"If everyone will just have a seat, I can take your questions one at a time. But first, let me address the violent attack on my son and daughter in law. After a thorough investigation, we have found that Kal Jansen, Chief Consular to my nephew, Aaron was responsible for the attack."

On the right side of the Aisle, Aaron stood quickly as if to object. But, he turned in what looked like an attempt to flee. He didn't get very far as security was waiting for him.

Next to me, Xander sat perfectly calm. "You knew this was going to happen?"

He squeezed my hand. "Yeah. His people were arrested this morning. But my mother wanted to make an example of him in front of cameras to send a message."

"This is what you were doing all morning?

"I've been busy."

"I can see that."

Once Aaron was in cuffs, the room erupted into pure pandemonium. Reporters shouting questions. Flashbulbs going off. But security, was quick and efficient. One moment, Aaron was there, the next, he wasn't.

One by one, the new queen called on several people and answered questions clearly and concisely, having fully anticipated all the confusion. She was born ready.

I just looked at my husband. "When were you going to tell me?"

"I wanted it to be a surprise. Besides, you were right. We do everything together. And ruling, I would want to do it with you, but so much of it would sit on my shoulders. There would be so much time that I'd be spending with advisors and not with my family. If I could rule by committee, with you and Alexi and Abbie with all of us having input, I could truly be great. But on my own, I don't make the best decisions."

"Of course you do. I trust you implicitly. My only concern is when you convince yourself that you're all alone. Then you make rash decisions."

"I know. The point is, we just had a baby. And she's had a tough go of it. I want to be able to sit around and play with her and not have to worry about who's coming to kill her because they want her throne. I want her to have as normal a life as possible. Besides, there was a lot of ego that went into my decision to succeed my mother. I did it because I thought I was protecting Lex, that I was doing the best thing. But it's not the best thing. I'm not cut out for this. But Derrick is someone who could be."

"You're amazing."

He shook his head. "No. You are. You are and always have been my queen. Don't ever doubt that. But you deserve normal and happy, and that's what I can give you by abdicating."

"Let me just say, you are hardly normal."

He grinned. "Well, normal with a little bit of flair, because it *is* still me."

I laughed. Kaya waved a fist in the air and cooed. Xander leaned forward and kissed her little hand as she gave him a gassy smile. "You see that? My daughter smiled at me."

"It was gas, Xander."

He pshawed at me. "You don't know. My daughter and I are super connected. She gets me."

I just laughed. And he leaned forward, brushing his lips over mine. "You know what today is, right?"

I frowned. "What?"

"Today is sex day."

I laughed. "Is it?"

"You know you've been counting down too."

I knew exactly what day it was, but I wasn't telling him that.

"So when we're done here, and the press has asked all the questions and crowded you and my baby, we're going to hand her to the nanny, and I'm going to fuck my wife. Then we'll talk about all the things that have happened. How does that sound?"

"Fuck first, talk later?"

He grinned. "Now you're getting it. I love you so much."

"You're impossible. And I wouldn't have you any other way."

"Awesome. So, you just think about what position you'd like to start with, because I have my favorites. But God, I have a lot of pent-up frustration here."

I could only laugh as I stroked his face and held our daughter. I couldn't imagine a more perfect life. My husband loved me enough to give up a crown. I didn't know what more I could ask for.

👑

THANK YOU FOR READING PLAYBOY's HEART, THE conclusion to the Playboy Prince Duet. The deliciously sexy thrill ride doesn't end here though! After all, London is full of alpha Billionaires with secrets to protect and vengeance to deliver.

*It began with **betrayal**.*
*And ended in **murder**.*

She was never supposed to cross my path.
*She was never supposed to know about the **Currency of Secrets** or the **Oaths of Blood**.*

My so-called brothers killed my friend. *I intend to make them pay. And before it's over, I'll bend all the rules of morality, decency and legality. I will borrow and steal to set the scales right.*

My name is Ben Covington and I know my sins.

Order Big Ben now!

Need another edge of your seat romance right this instant? Try my epic bodyguard romance with a sexy as sin military hero in, PROTECTING THE HEIRESS!

Read Protecting the Heiress NOW!

*"...a **dramatic, suspenseful and amazing read** that you just can't put down. I loved it!"*———**Sue, Goodreads Reviewer**

Can't get enough billionaires? Meet a cocky, billionaire prince that goes undercover in Cheeky Royal! He's a prince with a secret to protect. The last distraction he can afford is his gorgeous as sin new neighbor.
His secrets could get them killed, but still, he can't stay away...

Read Cheeky Royal now!

Turn the page for an excerpt from Cheeky Royal…

UPCOMING BOOKS

Big Ben
The Benefactor
For Her Benefit
East End
East Bound
Fall of East

"You make a really good model. I'm sure dozens of artists have volunteered to paint you before."

He shook his head. "Not that I can recall. Why? Are you offering?"

I grinned. "I usually do nudes." Why did I say that? It wasn't true. Because you're hoping he'll volunteer as tribute.

He shrugged then reached behind his back and pulled his shirt up, tugged it free, and tossed it aside. "How is this for nude?"

Fuck. Me. I stared for a moment, mouth open and looking like an idiot. Then, well, I snapped a picture. Okay fine, I snapped several. "Uh, that's a start."

He ran a hand through his hair and tussled it, so I snapped several of that. These were romance-cover gold. Getting into it, he started posing for me, making silly faces. I got closer to him, snapping more close-ups of his face. That incredible face.

Then suddenly he went deadly serious again, the intensity in his eyes going harder somehow, sharper. Like a razor. "You look nervous. I thought you said you were used to nudes."

I swallowed around the lump in my throat. "Yeah, at school whenever we had a model, they were always nude. I got used to it."

He narrowed his gaze. "Are you sure about that?"
Shit. He could tell. "Yeah, I am. It's just a human form. Male. Female. No big deal."

His lopsided grin flashed, and my stomach flipped. Stupid traitorous body...and damn him for being so damn good looking. I tried to keep the lens centered on his face, but I had to get several of his abs, for you know...research.
But when his hand rubbed over his stomach and then slid to the button on his jeans, I gasped, "What are you doing?"
"Well, you said you were used doing nudes. Will that make you more comfortable as a photographer?"

I swallowed again, unable to answer, wanting to know what he was doing, how far he would go. And how far would I go?

The button popped, and I swallowed the sawdust in my mouth. I snapped a picture of his hands.

Well yeah, and his abs. So sue me. He popped another button, giving me a hint of the forbidden thing I couldn't have. I kept snapping away. We were locked in this odd, intimate game of chicken. I swung the lens up to capture his face. His gaze was slightly hooded. His lips parted...turned on. I stepped back a step to capture all of him. His jeans loose, his feet bare. Sitting on the stool, leaning back slightly and giving me the sex face, because that's what it was— God's honest truth—the sex face. And I was a total goner.

"You're not taking pictures, Len." His voice was barely above a whisper.

"Oh, sorry." I snapped several in succession. Full body shots, face shots, torso shots. There were several torso shots. I wanted to fully capture what was happening.
He unbuttoned another button, taunting me, tantalizing me. Then he reached into his jeans, and my gaze snapped to meet his. I wanted to say something. Intervene in some way...help maybe...ask him what he was doing. But I

couldn't. We were locked in a game that I couldn't break free from. Now I wanted more. I wanted to know just how far he would go.

Would he go nude? Or would he stay in this half-undressed state, teasing me, tempting me to do the thing that I shouldn't do?

I snapped more photos, but this time I was close. I was looking down on him with the camera, angling so I could see his perfectly sculpted abs as they flexed. His hand was inside his jeans. From the bulge, I knew he was touching himself. And then I snapped my gaze up to his face.
Sebastian licked his lip, and I captured the moment that tongue met flesh.

Heat flooded my body, and I pressed my thighs together to abate the ache. At that point, I was just snapping photos, completely in the zone, wanting to see what he might do next.

"Len..."
"Sebastian." My voice was so breathy I could barely get it past my lips.
"Do you want to come closer?"
"I--I think maybe I'm close enough?"

His teeth grazed his bottom lip. "Are you sure about that? I have another question for you."

I snapped several more images, ranging from face shots to shoulders, to torso. Yeah, I also went back to the hand-around-his-dick thing because…wow. "Yeah? Go ahead." "Why didn't you tell me about your boyfriend 'til now?" Oh shit. "I—I'm not sure. I didn't think it mattered. It sort of feels like we're supposed to be friends." Lies all lies. He stood, his big body crowding me. "Yeah, friends…" I swallowed hard. I couldn't bloody think with him so close. His scent assaulted me, sandalwood and something that was pure Sebastian wrapped around me, making me weak. Making me tingle as I inhaled his scent. Heat throbbed between my thighs, even as my knees went weak. "Sebastian, wh—what are you doing?"
"

Proving to you that we're not friends. Will you let me?" He was asking my permission. I knew what I wanted to say. I understood what was at stake. But then he raised his hand and traced his knuckles over my cheek, and a whimper escaped.

His voice went softer, so low when he spoke, his words were more like a rumble than anything intelligible. "Is that you telling me to stop?"

Seriously, there were supposed to be words. There were. But somehow I couldn't manage them, so like an idiot I shook my head.

His hand slid into my curls as he gently angled my head. When he leaned down, his lips a whisper from mine, he whispered, "This is all I've been thinking about."
Read Cheeky Royal now!

NANA MALONE READING LIST

Looking for a few Good Books? Look no Further

FREE
Shameless
Before Sin
Cheeky Royal

Royals
Royals Undercover

Cheeky Royal
Cheeky King

Royals Undone
Royal Bastard

Bastard Prince

Royals United
Royal Tease
Teasing the Princess

Royal Elite

The Heiress Duet
Protecting the Heiress
Tempting the Heiress

The Prince Duet
Return of the Prince
To Love a Prince

The Bodyguard Duet
Billionaire to the Bodyguard
The Billionaire's Secret

London Royals

London Royal Duet
London Royal
London Soul

Playboy Royal Duet
Royal Playboy
Playboy's Heart

The Donovans Series
Come Home Again (Nate & Delilah)
Love Reality (Ryan & Mia)
Race For Love (Derek & Kisima)
Love in Plain Sight (Dylan and Serafina)
Eye of the Beholder – (Logan & Jezzie)
Love Struck (Zephyr & Malia)

London Billionaires Standalones
Mr. Trouble (Jarred & Kinsley)
Mr. Big (Zach & Emma)
Mr. Dirty(Nathan & Sophie)

The Shameless World

Shameless
Shameless
Shameful
Unashamed

Force
Enforce

Deep

Deeper

Before Sin

Sin

Sinful

Brazen

Still Brazen

The Player

<u>Bryce</u>

<u>Dax</u>

<u>Echo</u>

<u>Fox</u>

<u>Ransom</u>

<u>Gage</u>

The In Stilettos Series

<u>*Sexy in Stilettos (Alec & Jaya)*</u>

<u>*Sultry in Stilettos (Beckett & Ricca)*</u>

<u>*Sassy in Stilettos (Caleb & Micha)*</u>

<u>*Strollers & Stilettos (Alec & Jaya & Alexa)*</u>

<u>*Seductive in Stilettos (Shane & Tristia)*</u>

<u>*Stunning in Stilettos (Bryan & Kyra)*</u>

~ ~ ~

In Stilettos Spin off
Tempting in Stilettos (Serena & Tyson)
Teasing in Stilettos (Cara & Tate)
Tantalizing in Stilettos (Jaggar & Griffin)

Love Match Series
*Game Set Match (Jason & Izzy)
Mismatch (Eli & Jessica)

ABOUT NANA MALONE

USA Today Best Seller, Nana Malone's love of all things romance and adventure started with a tattered romantic suspense she "borrowed" from her cousin.

It was a sultry summer afternoon in Ghana, and Nana was a precocious thirteen. She's been in love with kick butt heroines ever since. With her overactive imagination, and channeling her inner Buffy, it was only a matter a time before she started creating her own characters.

Now she writes about sexy royals and smokin' hot body-guards when she's not hiding her tiara from Kidlet, chasing a puppy who refuses to shake without a treat, or begging her husband to listen to her latest hairbrained idea.

Printed in Poland
by Amazon Fulfillment
Poland Sp. z o.o., Wrocław